The Hound of
the Baskervilles

First published in 2003 by Usborne Publishing Ltd,
Usborne House, 83-85 Saffron Hill,
London EC1N 8RT, England.
www.usborne.com

A catalogue record for this title is available
from the British Library.

ISBN 07945 0574 0

Printed in Great Britain

Series editors: Jane Chisholm and Rosie Dickins
Designed by Brian Voakes
Series designer: Mary Cartwright
Cover: Glen Bird

The Hound of the Baskervilles

from the story by
Sir Arthur Conan Doyle
retold by Henry Brook

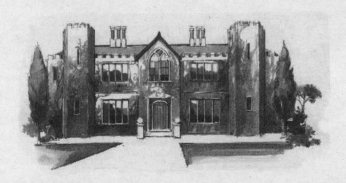

Illustrated by Bob Harvey

Contents

About The Hound of the Baskervilles

First published in book form in 1902, this thrilling adventure of a monstrous hound preying on the heirs of the Baskerville fortune has many claims to fame. Not least because it is the best-known case of the world's greatest fictional detective, Mr. Sherlock Holmes. But his involvement in the Baskerville investigation only came about by chance. If Conan Doyle hadn't changed his mind at the last moment, we might never have heard of Holmes again.

Conan Doyle had created the brilliant sleuth, who lived at 221b Baker Street, while he was earning a modest income as a doctor. In the space of a few years, the stories had made him famous and rich, but the author confessed to his friends that he regarded the character as an unwelcome burden. Instead, he wanted to concentrate on writing historical novels, which he considered more important than the contemporary adventures of his London detective. So, in *The Adventure of the Final Problem* (1893), Conan Doyle had sent Holmes to his doom at the hands of his archenemy, Professor Moriarty. At the end of the story, both men plunge into the Reichenbach Falls, a thundering waterfall of "seething foam", high in the Swiss Alps.

But news of the detective's death shocked the country. City traders in London wore black ribbons in their hats, to mourn the loss of their beloved hero, and 20,000 Holmes' fans – known as Sherlockians – cancelled their subscriptions to *The Strand Magazine*, which had published the stories for the previous eighteen months. Despite all entreaties from the public, Conan Doyle was adamant: there would be no more Holmes stories.

Eight years later, a young journalist friend named "Bobbles" Robinson told him the legend of a ghost dog which stalked the lonely moorland of his home county of Devon. Conan Doyle immediately saw the potential for a new novel. He visited the maximum security prison on the moor, and toured the wild landscape of bogs and rocky cliffs.

But the writer still needed a powerful central character to strengthen the story, and so he turned to his most popular creation, the Baker Street investigator. He didn't revive him from his watery grave – though he would be forced to do so by his readers, a year later – so Watson narrates the story as one of their old cases. Whether Conan Doyle knew it or not, the decision to use Holmes helped make his new book a classic.

Sherlock Holmes was a man of his times, and those times were full of change. He lived in the capital city of the vast British empire, at the end of the Victorian era. This had been a confident period of British history, and had seen great achievements in exploration, art and science. Above all, it had produced the peculiarly British idea of "the gentleman": educated, refined, and with a rock-solid sense of duty and good-conduct. But this era was coming to a close. It was not only the growing social problems of poverty and crime that undermined the idea of a "gentlemanly society". There was the prospect of war looming in South Africa, as the empire began to crumble, and the impatient drive of new technology. Soon, the first cars would be rumbling through the streets. Communications were improving, with the advent of the telegram, an efficient postal service and the telephone. Even the night was being tamed: Thomas Edison invented a "long-life" electric lightbulb in 1879. The use of gas lamps and horse-drawn taxi cabs in Holmes' London was coming to an end.

But Dartmoor was a long way from London, in distance and in mind. The moor was still a remote and rural community, its wild landscape unchanged for centuries. This land of legends takes the reader back to an age of magic and wonder, but also to a time when people lived in darkness and fear. The possibility that this fear could return to haunt us in our modern world is what makes *The Hound of the Baskervilles* so terrifying.

Standing between the opposing forces of past and future is Sherlock Holmes. In his battle with the ghost dog, and the ancient savagery it represents, he must protect the new world of science and logic that he so passionately supports. At the same time, in his efforts to catch a ruthless murderer, he is acting as guardian for the old-world values of the gentleman. Holmes is honest, fearless and always fights to uphold the law, even when his life – or that of his closest friend, Watson – is threatened. There is no mention of a reward or any payment offered to the detective in this story. Holmes struggles with the bloodthirsty hound because he believes it is his duty.

Great books survive because they contain ideas and characters which we can recognize in our own times. Like Holmes, we all have to balance a sense of the past with our vision of the future. This is what makes *The Hound of the Baskervilles* an enduring classic.

The Science of Deduction

I am not usually a nervous man, but last night I woke screaming. Something was pressing down on my throat, choking me.

It was the hound, snarling and tearing at my skin. I fought with it, but as my eyes adjusted to the gloom, I saw it was only the covers of my bed that I was struggling with. In the nightmare, I had thrashed so wildly, I had become tied in my own sheets.

I could not go back to sleep after dreaming of the beast

on the moor. I dressed and went down to my study, to look over the files of some patients, in preparation for my morning clinic. But I was in no mood to concentrate on work. All I could think of was the strange series of events which ended with that terrible encounter in the fog.

And so I decided the time had come for me to write down the facts of Mr. Sherlock Holmes' most amazing adventure: The Hound of the Baskervilles.

It began, as so many of our investigations did, with a mysterious visitor to our rented rooms at 221b Baker Street. We were two bachelors, Holmes and I, who had decided to share the costs of a London apartment.

My story before then was a simple one. I had joined the British army as a young man and trained as a doctor. In my first year of service I was sent out to India, where I was promptly shot in the left shoulder during the disastrous battle of Maiwand. My recovery from the enemy bullet might have been a speedy one, but while in the hospital I came down with a tropical fever that ravaged me for months. I was not expected to survive.

However, I finally mustered enough strength to take a troopship home to Portsmouth, and having no family or other attachments, I soon drifted to London, that great magnet for idlers and loungers and those who are simply "not sure what to do next" with their lives. I was introduced to Sherlock Holmes by a medical acquaintance. Holmes had been using his hospital's laboratory to conduct some chemical experiments and had mentioned he was looking for someone to share an apartment.

When we first moved in we were strangers, but slowly a bond of friendship grew between us. Still weak from the fever, I had no job and was living on a small pension from the army. Years later, I would marry and set up my own medical practice. But, in the meantime, in Baker Street, I had lots of spare time to help my new friend with his strange occupation. He described himself as "an investigator of puzzles", and Baker Street was his office as well as our comfortable home. People came to seek Holmes' help when all other attempts to solve their problems had failed. When the police were baffled and danger was close by, when hope was almost gone, it was then that they would come knocking at our door.

It was a dreary, rain-lashed October afternoon in the year 1889, if I remember correctly. There had been no cases of interest for several weeks. Holmes was stretched out in his armchair, surrounded by piles of crumpled newspapers.

"Nothing, Watson. No news. Not so much as a lost cat. All the criminals of London have packed their bags and left the city."

I knew how my friend suffered from boredom if he wasn't working on a case. His mind was the sharpest in the country and needed constant activity. Without a challenge, he was like a champion race horse, kept locked in its stable.

"Nothing in the papers then?" I asked.

"There hasn't been for weeks. My one chance of amusement depends on meeting with the owner of this curious object." He was balancing a walking stick across his hands. It was made from a fine, thick piece of blackwood. The head was bulbous and, at its neck, I could see a wide, silver band glinting in the light from the fire.

"Where did you find that, Holmes?"

"By the coal bucket. Mrs. Hudson let a gentlemen in to wait for us, when we were out dining yesterday afternoon. But he hurried off before we returned, forgetting his cane."

"A client?" I asked, excitedly.

"I certainly hope so, Watson. Well, what do you make of it?" He held the stick out for me to examine. It was heavy and worn with use. There were some words stamped onto the silver: *To Dr. James Mortimer, from his friends at the C.C.H. 1884*

"Here's a rainy-day game for you to play, Watson," said Holmes, with a chuckle. "What can you tell me about our Dr. Mortimer, from a study of his cane?"

"Very well," I answered, accepting the challenge. "He is an elderly, country doctor, well-respected. The stick was given to him on his retirement, perhaps by

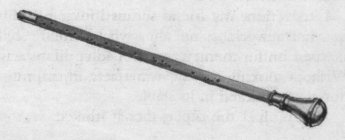

his local hunting club. He may have treated an injured rider, Holmes. That would explain the last letter of the 'C.C.H.' inscription. 'H' would stand for 'hunt', you see?"

"Anything else?" said Holmes, urging me on.

"No," I said confidently. "I think that's about everything we can discover."

"Excellent work, Watson." He reached over and took the stick from me. "I assume you saw how the wood is worn, and this was enough to convince you that our man lives in the country and walks about a lot? I would agree, and congratulate you. You have only missed a few little things."

"And what are they?"

Holmes smiled. "Oh, that he is a man in his early thirties, who did his medical training at a hospital in London, that he is friendly, not too ambitious about his work, absent-minded, and that he owns a medium-sized dog, perhaps a spaniel."

"Holmes," I cried. "How can you possibly tell all that, from examining a plain walking stick?"

"Elementary, Watson. It is common sense. Add to that, the science of deduction."

"I don't understand you, Holmes. I am not familiar with the term."

"Deduction, Watson. It means looking at all the facts in a puzzle, then deciding what is the most likely explanation for them. It is how I solve all my cases. I begin by looking closely at the facts, in this case, the stick I am holding..."

"But I had a good look at the stick too," I

protested, "and I didn't see all those things."

"You looked, but you didn't notice," he replied. "Tell me, Watson, how many steps are there, from the street entrance of this house, up to our rooms?"

"What are you talking about, Holmes?"

"You don't know, do you, Watson?"

"Now I think of it, no, I don't know – and it doesn't seem important, either."

"But it might be," he said quickly, "if a man's life were at stake. Every detail can be important if it helps to explain a puzzling case. There are eleven steps, Watson. I have trained my eyes not just to see things, but to notice all their details and remember them. I noticed that the stick is covered in small puncture marks."

"I saw them too. They are the scratches from loose stones or a scrape from a wall. What else could have caused them?"

"The sharp teeth of a loyal, medium-sized dog, that hurries after our mystery doctor on his country strolls. A large dog would have no difficulty in holding a heavy stick like this one, and a small dog would fail to lift it at all. A medium-sized dog could manage it, but would need to sink its teeth into the wood, to get a good grip. A spaniel is a popular breed in this size."

"Of course!" I said. "You know, once you explain it to me, it seems quite simple. But what about all the other things you suggested?"

"Think about the letters 'C.C.H.', my friend," he said, with a smile. "Now, what connects the letter 'H' with a doctor?"

"Hospital?" I blurted out.

"And one of the most famous London hospitals is called..."

"Charing Cross," I cried.

"Exactly."

Sherlock Holmes pressed his fingertips together and closed his eyes in concentration. He reminded me of one of my old medical school professors, giving a lecture. "Now, if our mystery man had worked all his life at this famous hospital in the heart of London, it is likely that he would have become an operating surgeon by the time of his retirement. But operating surgeons, as you should know, Watson, do not put 'Dr.' before their names. So, if he was still using the title 'Dr.', it is more likely that he trained at the hospital as a junior doctor, and was leaving to take up a new practice in the country. As the date on the stick is only five years ago, and his training would take about five years, I would suggest that he can only be in his early thirties, and is not an elderly gentleman, as you proposed. Now, Watson, how many ambitious London doctors would leave the capital city to start their practice?"

"None, Holmes," I said meekly.

"That explains my remark as to his lack of ambition. As for him being friendly, we know he made some firm friends at the hospital, because this is a good quality stick and must have been expensive. Men with lots of friends are usually friendly, are they not? And lastly, he must be an absent-minded fellow, if he can misplace such a valuable object in another man's home."

"Sometimes, Holmes," I said with a frown, "you seem to have almost supernatural powers."

"Not at all, my friend. I am quite human. All I use is my common sense and the science of deduction. I look at all the facts, I imagine all the possible solutions to the puzzle, and then I begin crossing them off. Whatever is left over, after all my tests, however unlikely it seems, must be the truth."

"And this is how you investigate your cases?"

"Exactly, Watson. And the next one is, if I am not mistaken, exactly halfway up the stairs."

"Holmes," I cried, "you have the ears of a fox."

"Only the ears of a bored detective, my friend... Come in, doctor."

The Curse

A tall, thin man with a nose like a beak entered our rooms and paced about in great excitement. His eyes were small and set close together. They sparkled and danced behind a pair of gold-rimmed glasses. He was dressed in a suit that was rather tired with wear, but he had the bearing of a gentleman. I guessed he was around thirty-five years of age.

"I am here on urgent business," said the man nervously. "My name is Dr. James Mortimer, and I must have your help."

"I will do my best," said Holmes, "if the case is an interesting one. Please be seated."

I gestured for our guest to sit down in one of the leather armchairs.

"I have in my pocket an old manuscript," the doctor announced, with a glance that showed he expected us to be impressed.

"Early 18th-century," stated Holmes, matter-of-factly. "If you call that old."

"But how could you know about the date, sir?"

"It is my business to know," said Holmes coolly. "Isn't that why you came?"

"I have heard something of your reputation. You are called the 'Master Detective' by criminal types, and an 'amateur nuisance' by the police. Some say you are the most brilliant man in the country. Others claim you are a fraud. But none of that tells me how you come to know the age of my manuscript."

Holmes smiled. "I do like to have a reputation, Watson. 'Master Detective' you say, Dr. Mortimer? Well, the 'Master Detective' can see a corner of your manuscript sticking out of your jacket pocket. I have good eyesight and I have studied historical writing. The style featured on your manuscript dates from around 1730."

"The exact date is 1742," said the doctor, looking a little annoyed. He settled back into his chair by the fire, drew the parchment from his pocket and offered it to Holmes. "This paper was entrusted to me by Sir Charles Baskerville, whose sudden and tragic death, some three months ago, caused such a shock in the county of Devon. I was his friend as well as his doctor. He was a strong man, practical and down to earth, as I am myself. But he still took this document seriously."

Holmes took the manuscript and flattened it across his knee. "You will observe, Watson," he said, at last looking interested in the discussion, "the peculiar length of the letter strokes. It is one of several clues which allowed me to fix the date."

I looked over his shoulder at the yellow paper and the faded ink. *"Baskerville Hall, 1742"* was written at the top.

"It appears to be a statement of some sort, Holmes."

"Of a certain legend," whispered the doctor, "which runs in the Baskerville family."

"I don't deal in legends," snapped Holmes. "I deal with facts and modern problems."

"This is a most modern problem," answered the doctor, with more force in his voice than I had expected from his spindly frame. "It must be solved within twenty-four hours, and there is a life at stake. This manuscript is short and directly connected with the affair. With your permission, I will read it to you."

Holmes nodded and leaned back in his chair. Once again, he placed his fingertips together and closed his eyes, an air of resignation settling across his features. Dr. Mortimer turned the paper to the light from the fire and began to read...

Much has been said about the legend of the Hound of the Baskervilles, and some believe it is only a story. But as I come in a direct line from Hugo Baskerville, and as I heard the legend from my father, who heard it from his, I have written it down believing it to be true.

In the time of the English Civil War, the Manor of Baskerville was owned by this Hugo, and he was by all accounts a mean, coarse and violent man. People might have forgiven him this, because the country around here is wild and desolate and breeds hard men. But Hugo was worse than hard. He had a mad streak in him.

It happened that Hugo fell in love with a farmer's daughter who lived near the Hall. The girl avoided him, scared off by his evil reputation. But Hugo was used to having what he wanted. So, one winter's day, he crept down to the girl's farm, with a gang of his thuggish friends, and kidnapped her. She was imprisoned in an attic room in Baskerville Hall, and Hugo and his friends sat down to a long drinking session to celebrate the capture. The desperate girl could hear the cursing and roaring of her admirer downstairs. In panic she clambered out onto the thick ivy which covered the walls of the house. When she had climbed down she ran onto the moor, heading for her family's farm, three miles distant.

But Hugo couldn't stay away from his captive for long. He went up to her room and, when he discovered that his prisoner had flown her cage, he stormed back downstairs and sprang upon the main table, glasses and plates flying before him. He cried out in front of the whole room that he would give his soul to hell, if only he could catch 'the wench'.

The drinkers stood open-mouthed at Hugo's mad fury. Then one of them shouted, 'Set the dogs after her!' Hugo ran out of the house, calling to his grooms to saddle his horse and fetch his hounds from the kennels. He gave the servant in charge of the hounds a handkerchief, which the girl had dropped in her flight, and told him to let the dogs sniff it to catch her scent. The pack tore off. Hugo mounted his mighty black stallion and chased after them, leaving his friends in confusion, drunkenly trying to clamber onto their horses.

At last they were ready to follow and, with the light of a full moon to guide them, they raced across the moor. They had gone a mile or two when they passed a shepherd, and they called to him, 'Have you seen our prey?' As the legend goes, the man was so crazed with fear that he could hardly speak. But at last he stammered that he had seen the girl and the hounds on her track. 'But I have seen more than that,' he went on, his voice shaking with fright. 'Hugo Baskerville passed me on his black stallion, and running right behind him was such a dark hound of hell as God forbid should ever come looking for me.'

Hugo's friends laughed and cursed the old shepherd as a fool. They rode on, into the night. But soon, their blood turned cold as they saw Hugo's mighty black horse galloping towards them, dappled with white froth. Its eyes were wide in panic – and its saddle was empty. But they were so drunk that they carried on regardless, ignoring even this second warning.

At last they found the pack of dogs, once a fierce hunting team, now a whimpering huddle at the entrance to a thin valley in the moor. Most of the men were too scared to ride down into this valley of fear, but the three bravest pushed on. The moon was shining bright upon the clearing and there before them was the poor girl, stretched out on the grass, dead of fear and fatigue.

But it was not the sight of her dead body, nor that of their friend Hugo Baskerville's lying next to it, which stopped their hearts beating in their chests. Towering over Hugo, and plucking at his throat, there stood a foul thing, a great, black beast, shaped like a hound, but larger than any hound that walks the daylight world. And, even as they watched, the thing tore out his throat.

When it turned its blazing, yellow eyes and dripping jaws towards them, the three cowards shrieked and rode for dear life, screaming as they went, fleeing across the moor.

One, it is said, died of his fright that same night. The other two were broken men for the rest of their lives.

This is the legend, my sons, of the coming of the hellhound which is said to have cursed our family ever since. Many of your ancestors have had sudden, bloody and mysterious deaths. And so I advise you to be cautious, and to avoid crossing the moor in those dark hours when the powers of evil are at their deadliest.

John Baskerville

When Dr. Mortimer had finished reading this shocking account, he pushed his gold-rimmed spectacles up onto his forehead and stared across at Sherlock Holmes. "What do you think of that, detective?"

Holmes yawned. "It is an old fairy tale," he said, waving one of his slender hands in dismissal.

Dr. Mortimer pulled another piece of paper out of his jacket pocket. "In that case, Mr. Holmes," he said quietly, "we will give you something a little more modern. This is a cutting from *The Devon County Chronicle* of the fourteenth of May of this year. It includes a short account of the death of Sir Charles Baskerville."

My friend leaned forward, his eyes suddenly alert, as the doctor began...

The recent death of Sir Charles has cast a gloom over the county. Sir Charles was generous and friendly, and determined to restore Baskerville Hall to its old glory. As is widely known, he made his fortune prospecting for gold in South Africa. He often gave considerable donations to local charities.

The circumstances connected with his death have not been entirely cleared up by the inquest. But enough has been done to dispose of those wild claims that have grown out of local superstition. There is no good reason to suspect foul play or accident.

Sir Charles' servants at the Hall consisted of a married couple called Barrymore, the husband acting as butler, and the wife as housekeeper and cook. Their evidence shows that Sir Charles' health had been failing for some time, and points especially to a problem with his heart. He suffered from hot flushes, breathlessness and bad nerves.

The facts of the death are simple. Sir Charles liked to walk down the famous yew tree avenue of Baskerville Hall every night before going to bed. On the fourth of May, Sir Charles had declared that he was leaving for London the next day. That night he went out as usual for his walk, in the course of which he would often smoke a cigar. He never returned.

At twelve o'clock, Barrymore, seeing the hall door was still open, became alarmed. Lighting a lamp, he went in search of his master. The day had been wet, and Sir Charles' footmarks were easily traced down the avenue. Halfway down is a gate which leads out to the open moor. There were signs that Sir Charles had stood here for some time.

> Barrymore proceeded down the avenue, and it was at the far end that his master's body was discovered. One fact which has not been explained is Barrymore's claim that Sir Charles' footprints changed in size and length of step from the time after he passed the moorgate. He appeared from there onwards to have been walking on his toes...

Holmes let out a snort at this. The doctor looked up and Holmes, without opening his eyes, waved a hand to indicate he should continue reading.

> Mr. Murphy, a gipsy horse-dealer, was nearby on the moor at the time, but he appears to have been drunk. He thinks he heard cries, but they were coming from the other end of the yew avenue, moving away from the house. No signs of violence were found on the body and, although the doctor's evidence mentioned an incredible facial distortion, this was explained as a common symptom of heart problems. The postmortem showed heart disease and the coroner recorded a verdict of death by natural causes.
>
> It is understood that the next of kin has been found: Mr. Henry Baskerville, the son of Sir Charles' younger brother. When last heard of, Henry Baskerville was raising cattle in a remote part of America, and he is at present being traced by local police, with a view to informing him of his good fortune.

Dr. Mortimer folded the newspaper cutting neatly and tucked it into his jacket.

"Those are the public facts, Mr. Holmes, in connection with the death of Sir Charles Baskerville."

"The public facts? Perhaps," said Holmes, with a

sparkle in his eye, "you had better give me the private ones."

"If I go on," whispered the doctor, "I should say that I am confessing something I have told to no one else. My reason for keeping silent at the coroner's inquiry is that a man of science, like myself, holds back from confirming a popular superstition."

"You may confide in us, good doctor," said Holmes. "Kings and queens have sat where you are sitting and told us their secrets. Words spoken in this room will go no further."

"Very well," he breathed, as though relieved that at last he could share his secret. "The moor is sparsely inhabited, and those who live near each other are thrown together for company, by necessity. For this reason I saw a lot of Sir Charles. With the exception of the reclusive Mr. Frankland, Mr. Stapleton, the butterfly expert of Merripit House, and his beautiful sister Beryl, there are no other civilized people for miles around. And as well as being a good friend, Sir Charles was my patient, and his illness made me a frequent visitor.

"Within the last few months, it became clear to me that his nervous system was strained to breaking point. He believed in the legend of the hound – so much so that, although he would walk in his own grounds, nothing could persuade him to go out on the moor at night. He was convinced that the curse was real.

"On more than one occasion he had asked me whether I had seen any strange creature out on the moor, or heard the baying of a hound. The latter question he asked me several times, always with a voice that vibrated with fear. I remember driving up to his house one evening, some three weeks before the fatal event.

"He was at his hall door. I had climbed down from my carriage and was standing in front of him, when I saw his eyes fix themselves over my shoulder and stare out into the dark with an expression of the most dreadful horror. I spun around just in time to see something which I thought must have been a large, black bull, passing at the top of the drive. He was so excited and alarmed that he made me go down to the spot where the animal had been and look around for it. It was gone, but the incident made him terribly nervous.

"I stayed with him all that evening, and he gave me the manuscript, to explain why he was so startled. I advised him to go to London. I knew his heart was dangerously weak and I thought that a few months among the distractions of the city would restore him to good health. But at the last moment came this terrible accident.

"On the night of his death, Barrymore sent Perkins, the groom, on horseback to fetch me. I reached Baskerville Hall within the hour. Following the footsteps down the yew avenue, I saw the spot where he had waited at the moor-gate, and then noticed the change in the footprints after this point. At last, I carefully examined the body.

"He lay on his face, his arms thrown out, his

fingers dug into the ground. His face was so twisted in horror that I found it difficult to identify him as my friend. But there was no physical injury of any kind. All the facts at the inquest were correct. Apart from one. Barrymore said there were no marks on the ground around the body. Perhaps he didn't see any. But I did, fresh and clear."

"Footprints?" asked Holmes, who was now staring intently at the doctor.

"Yes."

"Were they a man's or a woman's?" whispered my friend.

The country doctor looked strangely at us for a few seconds, his face lit by the flames flickering in the grate. When he spoke, I could barely hear him over the rain pounding on the window.

"Mr. Holmes, they were the footprints of a... a gigantic *hound*."

Sir Henry

I confess, at these words, a shudder passed through me. The doctor's face was full of terror. Holmes leaned forward in his excitement, and his eyes had the hard, dry sparkle which shot from them when he was fascinated by a case.

"You saw this?" he demanded.

"As clearly as I see you."

"But you said nothing at the inquest?"

"What was the use?" said the doctor, shaking his head.

"Why didn't anyone else see them?"

"They were some distance off from the body. If it hadn't been for my knowledge of the curse of the hellhound, I would never have made the connection, Mr. Holmes."

"Perhaps it was a sheepdog that made these marks?"

The doctor shook his head violently. "This was not a sheepdog. The prints were enormous."

"But it hadn't mauled the body," said Holmes quietly, as though deep in thought. "You said there was a gate out onto the moor. Was this the only way out from the yew tree avenue?"

"It is the only side exit. The trees of the avenue are so thick, they're impenetrable. At the head of the avenue is the hall door and at the other end is a summerhouse."

Holmes sat up excitedly. "Had Sir Charles reached this summerhouse?"

"No, he was some way off."

"And did you see any marks by the gate?"

"The ground was too churned up. But I could tell Sir Charles had stood there for ten or fifteen minutes."

"How could you know that?"

"Because I saw that the ash had dropped twice from his cigar."

Holmes clapped his hands together in excitement. "A man who shares some of our skills of deduction, Watson. This is evidently a case of extraordinary interest."

He jumped up from his chair, took his pipe from the mantelpiece and began stuffing it with the strong, dark tobacco he kept in a Persian slipper by the fireside.

"If only I had been there sooner, Watson. Those footprints are like the letters on a page to the eyes of a trained detective, but by now they will have been smudged by the rain and the marching feet of country policemen. Why didn't you call me sooner, Dr. Mortimer?"

The doctor lifted the palms of his hands in despair. "For a time, Mr. Holmes, I was not sure this was a case a common detective might be able to solve."

Holmes stopped filling his pipe suddenly. "You don't mean to say that you think the hound is supernatural? A ghost?"

"There is some monster out there, Mr. Holmes," said the doctor, clearly embarrassed. "Before the incident, a number of local farmers reported sightings of a giant beast" – he lowered his voice – "a *luminous* beast."

Holmes looked irritated by the doctor's words. "Luminous?" he snapped.

"They say its coat glows and terrible flames shoot from its mouth."

"And I thought you were a man of science," said Holmes coldly. "Why have you come to me then, if you believe we are dealing with... a demon?"

"Because, sir," answered the doctor, rising from his chair and taking out a watch, "in one hour and fifteen minutes, Sir Henry Baskerville will be getting off a train at Waterloo Station."

Holmes stroked his perfectly smooth chin. "The heir of the estate is arriving in London, then?"

"He is, and he is about to become a baronet. Sir Charles was the eldest of three brothers, all of whom are now dead. The title must pass to their children. The middle brother was Henry's father. He died a young man, soon after Henry was born. The youngest brother, Rodger, was the scoundrel of the family. I am told he was the spitting image of Sir Hugo, and just as wild. After a series of scandals in this country, he fled to Central America, where he died of yellow fever in 1876. He never married and he left no children."

"You are sure there is no other heir to the fortune?" asked Holmes, thoughtfully.

"Quite sure. Sir Henry is the last of the Baskervilles, and" − the doctor continued more loudly − "we must do all we can to protect him."

"Well, doctor, London is just as dangerous as Devon if we are dealing with a hellhound. The forces of evil are not confined to the country, are they? If you could visit me here at ten tomorrow morning with Sir Henry, I shall give you my thoughts on the matter. And please, say nothing to the heir until then."

"Very well," muttered the doctor, backing out of our room.

"Oh, by the way, Dr. Mortimer," said Holmes softly, "do you have a pet?"

"I do," he answered, mystified, "a dog, a little spaniel."

"Thank you," chuckled Holmes, "and don't forget this." He held the stick out to the retreating doctor, who nodded his head in thanks and departed.

"If you will excuse me, Watson," said Holmes reaching again for his tobacco store, "I require some time alone, to allow me to think."

I next saw Holmes late that evening, when I returned from a day spent relaxing at my club. He was in his dressing gown, coiled up in an armchair and puffing furiously on his pipe. A huge map lay spread across the floor in front of him.

"Watson, come look at Devon," he shouted, waving me over. He started pointing with his long, bony fingers. "You see, here is Baskerville Hall and the line of the yew tree avenue running to the summerhouse. There is Merripit House, where Mr. Stapleton and his sister live. This must be the small village of Grimpen. Fourteen miles away is Princetown prison for the criminally insane. And all around is the huge, lifeless moor. Now," he said, leaning back in his chair, "what do you make of this little case, dear fellow?"

"I don't really have a clue, Holmes," I admitted.

"Of course, but you are a man of action, Watson, better in a fight than at solving a puzzle. I, though, have spent all day examining the facts. What for instance, do you think of the curious change in Sir Charles' footprints?"

"Dr. Mortimer said that Sir Charles had tiptoed down that part of the avenue," I said, rather proud with myself for having remembered this fact.

"Only a fool would believe that, Watson."

"What then, Holmes?" I replied, slightly hurt.

"He was running, running for his life. He ran until his heart failed him."

"Running from what?"

"There is the mystery. The clue, my friend, is the

moor-gate. Mr. Murphy claims he heard cries moving away from the house. Why would Sir Charles run away from the house? He must have seen something that frightened him so badly that he lost his mind and ran, in panic, away from safety. The moor-gate must be our first clue." Holmes puffed thoughtfully on his pipe. Thick clouds of tobacco smoke soon filled the room, and I started to cough.

"Why would he be waiting there, Holmes?" I said, clearing my throat.

"And who for?" Holmes replied. "But these questions can wait till the morning. Pass me my violin, Watson, good chap. The case can be postponed until we meet the new owner of Baskerville Hall. For now, we shall surrender ourselves to music." And he began to play.

After Mrs. Hudson had cleared our breakfast table, Holmes retired to one of the armchairs. He lounged there in his dressing gown until our guests arrived, on the stroke of ten.

Sir Henry was a small but powerfully built man, of about thirty years of age. He had a strong and determined brow and, though I had heard he had been in the wilder regions of the earth, he gave the impression of being a gentleman. He was dressed in a rather strange suit of red tweed, with a matching cap. I wondered if these odd clothes were the fashion in the far-off Americas.

Dr. Mortimer introduced us all.

"You know it's strange, Mr. Holmes," said Sir

Henry in a light American accent, "if Mr. Mortimer hadn't told me he had an appointment with you this morning, I might have contacted you myself."

"Really?" said Holmes, his eyebrows curling with curiosity. "Why so?"

"Well, I have heard that you solve puzzles and mysteries, and I have a puzzle of my own."

For a moment I suspected the doctor had ignored Holmes' instruction to remain silent about his suspicions, but he looked as surprised as we did. Sir Henry took an envelope out of his pocket.

"It's probably a joke, but I can't say I find it very funny."

He quickly spread a piece of paper across our breakfast table with his big, weathered hands and we all peered at the curious message.

"Now," said Sir Henry Baskerville, "perhaps you will tell me, Mr. Holmes, what in thunder does that mean?"

"A puzzle indeed," said Holmes, inspecting the paper closely. "And not a supernatural one, would you say, Dr. Mortimer?"

"Supernatural?" barked Sir Henry. "You mean ghosts and things? It seems to me that you gentlemen know something you're not telling me. And I don't like being kept in the dark."

"Soon," said Holmes laying a calming hand on Sir Henry's shoulder, "you shall know everything. But first let us look at your note. Watson, fetch me *The Times* from yesterday if you will – the middle pages."

"I hardly think this is the appropriate moment to be relaxing with the papers," scoffed Dr. Mortimer. Holmes ignored this remark and took the requested pages from my hands. He began reading aloud, a long and peculiarly boring article about foreign trade and the price of rubber.

"Please, Mr. Holmes," interrupted Dr. Mortimer. "Have you lost your mind?"

"Far from it, I hope. But I have cracked our little puzzle, doctor."

"How so?"

"If you had listened to my speech, you might have heard the words 'you', 'value', 'keep away' and 'from the'. Do you perhaps recognize them?

"By thunder!" shouted Sir Henry. "My message."

"Quite," said Holmes, greatly pleased with himself. "I have already tried to explain to you, doctor, that I am an expert at recognizing certain facts and details. I have made it my business to do so."

"I suppose you mean the trick with my manuscript?" muttered Dr. Mortimer.

"I have mastered letter styles, as you have already seen, but these are only the tip of my mind's iceberg. I know all the different varieties of poisons and tobacco types. I can recognize the strands of thread from certain clothes, and even say where they were made and the name of the tailor who made them. I know all the types of soil that can be found around London. I know the world's ship schedules and railway timetables – and thousands of other similar facts. I have studied and memorized all these tiny pieces of information that most men consider unimportant. I have absorbed this information so that I can apply it to the science of deduction and investigation. You think me strange, but I am merely well-trained for my line of work. For example, doctor, I see a lump of mud on your shoe and I can make a good guess as to where you have been tramping in this great city. You took a walk in Regent's Park this morning, perhaps?"

"I did," the doctor whispered, considerably amazed.

"The red mud found around the lake is most distinctive."

"It must be," muttered the doctor.

"So do not be surprised if, when I see a piece of newspaper type, I can tell you from which paper it comes and from which individual section of that paper. Knowing these facts, eliminating all that is impossible and guessing what is likely, I come to the truth. Now be seated, gentlemen."

We took our chairs, spellbound, as Holmes continued talking.

"The note was composed in a hotel room in this city. The author had to write the word 'moor', as he found it difficult to find an example in the newspaper, and you can see that the ink is dry and unreliable. This is usually the case with hotel ink rather than ink found in private homes. I believe the note was written by someone who might have to show you their handwriting in the future and so hopes to disguise it, so it is quite possibly from someone you already know. I also believe that it was composed in a hurry. The words are clumsily pasted onto the paper. This indicates the composer feared an interruption at any second, but why and from whom

I do not know."

"Incredible," muttered the doctor. "You are a most unusual man. But I do feel you are relying on guesswork for these claims, not science."

"I choose the most likely explanation for the facts before me, doctor. You call it 'guesswork'. I would describe it as a 'scientific use of my imagination'."

The doctor tried to object, but Holmes ignored him. He picked up the message and examined it once more. He felt the paper and held it close to his face. Then he closed his eyes again. He looked like a man in a trance, or a sleepwalker who couldn't quite rouse himself from a dream.

"Tell me, Sir Henry," he said, suddenly back with us, "has anything else peculiar happened to you since you arrived in London?"

"Only some silliness with the hotel staff, but nothing important."

"Do go on," said Holmes, staring in interest.

"I seem to have lost a boot. I wouldn't mind so much, but I only bought the pair yesterday. Now one of them is missing. I needed some new things before I go down to Devon, you understand, Mr. Holmes?"

"I do. How peculiar to lose one boot."

"But that's enough about my wardrobe, gentlemen," said Sir Henry, rising from his chair. "It's time I heard what you have to tell of more important matters."

Sir Henry did not look so self-assured after he had listened to Dr. Mortimer's narrative. He shook his head in disbelief.

"I've heard the legend before, of course, but I thought it was all make-believe."

"Your safety is our first concern, Sir Henry," said Holmes. "Are you prepared to go to Baskerville Hall, while this danger lurks on the moor?"

Suddenly the baronet's face flushed red with rage and I realized he had inherited some of the legendary Baskerville temper.

"There is no devil in hell, Mr. Holmes," he growled, "and there is no man upon earth who could stop me from going back to my ancestral home. But I need some time to think this thing over. It's come as quite a surprise. Could you join us for lunch today at my hotel? By then, I should be feeling a little clearer about how best to proceed."

"Of course, Sir Henry," answered Holmes. "We shall be there at one o'clock exactly. May I call you a cab?"

"I'd prefer to walk. It might be a good idea to clear my head with some fresh air, after hearing such stories."

"I will join you, if I may," added the doctor.

So we saw our visitors to the door. As it closed behind them, I turned to my friend, ready to ask him about the strange developments in the case, but I was amazed to see him dashing to the coat stand for his overcoat and deerstalker hat. He seized my greatcoat and bundled me into it, ignoring my protests.

"Quick, Watson..."

"But I don't understand..."

"Hurry, man, explanations can come later. The game's afoot."

And we were out on the stairs in seconds, in hot pursuit.

I could see the two men strolling a few hundred yards ahead of us, making their way slowly down Baker Street.

"Should we catch up with them, Holmes?" I asked, rather confused. "Have you forgotten to ask them about something?"

"Quiet, Watson," whispered my friend, "I think I have him."

Sir Henry and the doctor were stopping now and again to look in at the shop windows that decorate the streets of London. I followed Holmes' stare. A hansom cab was rolling along just behind them, halting whenever they did.

"Come, Watson. Let's take a closer look at our spy."

He began crossing the street towards the cab. Suddenly, I glimpsed a shadowy face in the passenger compartment, a long, black beard and fierce yellow eyes blazing at us. Then the top of the cab flew open, our spy shouted a command and the horses tore off at full gallop.

Holmes looked desperately around for another cab, but there were none to be seen.

"Foiled, Watson," he snapped, "and all because I was too hasty."

Upon arrival at the Northumberland Hotel a few hours later, we could hear Sir Henry out on the landing, shouting at the top of his voice.

"I won't stand for it you hear? Get me the manager. Are you playing me for some kind of sucker?"

We ran up the central staircase, sure that our friend was being threatened, only to find him standing in the hallway, clasping an old, dusty leather boot in one hand, and a trembling valet in the other. Once again the baronet's face was crimson with rage, and his words were almost indistinguishable due to the anger in his voice.

"Where's the other one?" he yelled, and the valet raised his hands in fright.

"I have searched the entire hotel and I can't find it anywhere, sir."

"That's not good enough," barked Sir Henry. "Yesterday, I lost a new boot. Today, I lose an old one.

I want an explanation. Fetch me the manager."

Holmes stood stroking his chin as I tried to calm the furious baronet.

"To lose one boot would be unfortunate," muttered Holmes, "but to lose two..."

"It is the strangest thing, is it not?" seethed Sir Henry, overhearing him. "First, they take a brand new boot, and now I lose one of my old, trusty American pair, that were due to be thrown out. I don't understand it, sir."

"Strange indeed," agreed Holmes.

"Well, enough of this," said Sir Henry, releasing the waiter. "I won't let this spoil my whole day. Let's go downstairs and have some lunch. I'll talk to the manager later. I still have one pair of shoes left to wear."

After a sumptuous lunch, Sir Henry cleared his throat and made an announcement.

"Gentlemen, I have been thinking things over all morning and have made my decision. Whatever the dangers I must face, I prefer to face them than to run from them. I will travel to Baskerville Hall at the end of this week."

"I applaud your decision," said Holmes. "There is danger for you in the city. I assume you know that you were followed this morning."

The two men jumped to their feet.

"By whom?" demanded the doctor.

"A rascal with a thick, black beard. Is there anyone who sports a beard living in the vicinity of Baskerville Hall, doctor?"

"Why... Barrymore, the butler, does. But he has been with the family for four generations. Sir Charles trusted him completely. He and his wife received five hundred pounds each in the will."

"Aha," cried Holmes.

"I hope you don't suspect all those who received money, Mr. Holmes," said the doctor, sheepishly. "I myself received a thousand."

"Sir Charles was generous."

"He was also extremely rich. His estate was worth almost a million pounds."

"And who, if you will forgive the impertinence of the question, Sir Henry, would stand to gain as the next heir?"

"Since Rodger Baskerville died without children," answered the doctor, "the estate would go to a distant cousin."

"Really," exclaimed Holmes.

"He is a retired bishop, of saintly reputation. And a man who has already turned down the money left to him by Sir Charles."

"I see. And have you made a new will, Sir Henry?"

"I have not. I want the money to go to the repair and restoration of the Baskerville estate – but I intend to be around to see it happen."

"Well spoken. Perhaps in Devon your mystery

assailants will be driven into the open."

"I hope you'll be coming with me on this adventure, Mr. Holmes?"

"Sadly not," Holmes replied.

The doctor and Sir Henry were clearly shocked by Holmes' refusal.

"I am held in London by a delicate case of blackmail. I could not possibly leave the city, even for a day or two."

"Well then, we go together," said Sir Henry to Dr. Mortimer.

"But Dr. Mortimer has his patients to look after," said Holmes. "Fine man that he is, he will not be much protection. You need a sturdy man by your side, a man you can trust in any situation, no matter how dangerous." Holmes patted me on the arm. "I was hoping you, Watson, might accompany the doctor and Sir Henry, if you are not too busy?"

The baronet rushed over to my chair and shook my hand. "That's great news," he said excitedly. "I can see you're an old military man, Watson, from the way you carry yourself. You must have faced great dangers in the past. Will you come down to Baskerville Hall and see this one through with me?"

The promise of adventure has always fascinated me, and I was complimented by Holmes' words and Sir Henry's eagerness to accept me as his companion.

"It would be a pleasure," I declared.

Back in Baker Street, I made preparations for my departure while Holmes seemed distracted and restless. There was a sudden, heavy knock at our door.

"At last," Holmes shouted.

"But who is it?"

"You did not think me such an idiot that I should let the cab slip away without a clue, Watson. Come in, driver," he shouted.

A rough looking man strode into the room. "Who's been asking 'bout me then?" he said, gruffly. "They told me down the yard some toff's been asking after my cab. What's the complaint?"

"No complaint," said Holmes. "I have a half-sovereign for you if you can answer a few questions."

The driver smiled. "My lucky day with gentlemen and their sovereigns. Go on then."

"I saw your cab earlier today, on Baker Street."

"That's right," the man nodded.

"Tell me about your fare."

"He was a gentleman like you, well-dressed, long beard, wanted to follow a couple of blokes around town for the day. He said he was a detective."

"Indeed? What else did he tell you?"

"Nothing much. He mentioned his name of course."

Holmes jumped up, shooting a look of triumph over at me. "That was foolish, with me on his tracks, Watson." He turned back to the cab driver. "What name was it?"

"His name," said the cab driver, "was Mr. Sherlock Holmes."

Never have I seen my friend so completely amazed. For a second he was mute with surprise, then he roared with laughter.

"One to him, Watson, one to him. He is, I believe, a worthy adversary for my talents."

Holmes paid the driver, who had no other information about the mystery man, and we were left alone in our rooms, with the fire crackling in the grate. I could see Holmes had something he wanted to say to me, and I watched the flames in silence, waiting for him to begin. Finally, he spoke.

"You must be careful down there without me, Watson. Our opponent is a cunning and ruthless man. He has beaten me in London. He guessed that I would trace his driver – easy enough to find from the description of the horses and the style of the cab, and easier still when a few drivers owe you a good turn. He knew I would ask for a description of the customer, so he sent back this challenge to me. He is bold, Watson." He turned to me from the firelight. "You may smile, but I give you my word that I shall be very glad to have you back, safe and sound in Baker Street."

Baskerville Hall

On the way to Waterloo Station, Holmes gave me his final instructions.

"Remember, Watson, you are my eyes and ears down there at Baskerville Hall. Send me daily reports with all the information you discover. Don't try to solve the case yourself. Send me all the facts, and let me do the brainwork here in London."

"What facts exactly?"

"Anything at all that might have a bearing on the case. Descriptions of the locals and their activities might be useful. Remember that the smallest piece of information you supply might lead to the solution of the puzzle."

"Very well, Holmes. I shall do my best not to disappoint you."

As we stopped at the station entrance, he put his hand on my arm. "You do have your revolver with you, don't you Watson?" I was comforted to see that he said these words with a look of concern for me, as his friend.

"Ghost dog or not, I thought it wise to bring it along."

"Keep it with you, day and night. And never allow Sir Henry to go out onto the moor, unless you are by his side."

Our friends were already waiting for us at the platform for West Country trains. Holmes made his apologies again, for the serious case that prevented his coming with us on the adventure. Then he wished us the best of luck. Just as we were about to board, he called out: "Bear in mind, Sir Henry, the advice from the manuscript. At all costs, avoid the moor in the hours of darkness."

I watched his tall, angular figure gazing after us, shrinking into the distance as our train chugged out of the station.

In a few hours, it was as though we were in another country. There were no buildings or other signs of development, only wide valleys dotted with granite rocks and a few cows grazing in lush, thick-hedged fields. The rich grass was a sign that, since leaving the cold, smoggy streets of London, we had entered a warmer and damper climate. I noticed that Sir Henry was shifting around in his seat, studying the passing countryside with great excitement.

"I've not seen Devon since I was a boy of thirteen, but I always remembered how beautiful it was."

"Have you ever seen the Hall?" I asked him.

"My father had a little cottage a hundred miles south of the Baskerville estate, and when he died, I was shipped straight off to America. I've never seen the Hall, or the famous moor that surrounds it."

The doctor leaned over. "There is your moor, Sir Henry," he announced proudly.

In the distance, I saw a melancholy hill with a ridge of jagged peaks, dim and vague, like the landscape from a dream. Beyond this was a dark plateau, a plain that stretched off to the horizon. I wondered what dangers might lie in wait for us there, and I missed Holmes, who had always guided me through our adventures in the past. Sir Henry remained silent for a few minutes, as though hypnotized by this first sighting of his ancient homeland.

After a half day's travel, we stopped at the small station of Coombe Tracey, a village in the bottom of a wooded valley. It was a pretty and peaceful-looking place, but I was surprised to see two soldiers posted at the station gate. They were leaning on their short rifles, and they studied us keenly as we left the platform.

An open carriage was waiting for us. In a few moments our luggage was loaded and we were flying along the narrow road with the wind beating in our faces. On either side there were fields and little woods, and a few comfortable-looking cottages peeping out from among the thick, green foliage. It was a crisp, bright afternoon, but beyond the lushness of the valley, there rose the dark, gloomy curve of the high moor, towering above us.

We began to climb out of the valley, clattering over gushing streams and disturbing great mounds of fallen leaves. Suddenly, as we turned a sharp corner in the road, the coachman pulled hard on the reins and our carriage skidded to a halt. In the middle of the track there was a mounted soldier, with a stern face and a rifle resting across his arm.

"Hello – what's going on here?" cried Dr. Mortimer.

The soldier came over, glanced into our carriage, then waved the driver on. After we had rounded the bend, the driver turned to us.

"It's the convict," he shouted, "escaped last week from Princetown. The army has been called in to catch him."

"That seems rather excessive," said the doctor.

"Aye, but this is no ordinary prisoner, sir. It's Selden on the loose."

"*Selden...*" the doctor gasped.

I took a deep breath and felt inside my overcoat for the reassuring bulge of my revolver. That name was enough to drive fear into the strongest heart. Selden was the notorious Notting Hill strangler, only saved from the hangman's noose because his crimes were so ferocious and bloodthirsty that the jury had doubted he could be completely sane.

We climbed over the rim of the valley and onto the vast, rolling plain of the moor. Huge boulders were scattered across it, and the wind grew so cold that we all pulled our overcoats closer around us. Somewhere out on that desolate heath was Selden, hiding like a hunted, savage beast. The thought made me shiver.

"There it is, sir," called the coachman. "Baskerville Hall."

At first, all we could see were two dark towers hanging above a dip in the moor. Then we turned down into a driveway and a long avenue of trees. Sir Henry sat up in the carriage, with flushed cheeks and shining eyes.

"Was it here that it happened?" he whispered.

"No," said the doctor in a timid voice. "The yew tree avenue is on the other side of the hall."

Glimmering and ghost-like at the end of that long, dark driveway was a huge stately home built of black granite. It was covered in ivy and I could see arrow slits and narrow windows, hidden in the tangle of green. A man was waiting for us, standing in the

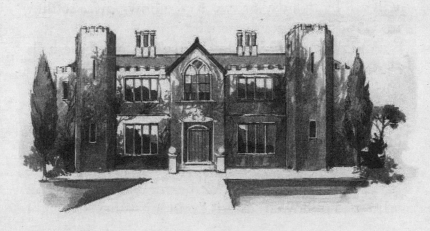

shadow of a massive oak door.

"Welcome, Sir Henry. Welcome to Baskerville Hall."

He took our bags and vanished into the house. We stepped into an entrance hall not much changed for five hundred years or more. It was a huge space, lit only by a few sputtering candles and the embers of a fire glowing in a great, old-fashioned fireplace. Our shadows were tall and spindly across the wood-panelled walls. High above us, the windows were dark and partly covered by heavy, velvet curtains that stretched down to the stone floor. The furniture was made of thick, age-blackened oak, and there was a line of shadowy portraits arranged above the fireplace and running off into the gloom.

"I must leave you now," said the doctor, waiting at the doorway. "I have patients to see."

"You won't stay for dinner?" asked Sir Henry, a touch nervously I thought.

"No, but you may summon me at any time, and I will call by in a day or two to see how you're settling in. Good night, gentlemen."

And so we were left in the dark heart of the hall.

"Sort of spooky, isn't it?" whispered Sir Henry.

"A little," I answered, thinking that this house would terrify the bravest of men.

"Will you be taking dinner?" It was the butler, who had appeared in the room without making a sound. He was around forty years old, tall and handsome, with a full, black beard. Was this the man who had followed us in London? What secrets, I wondered, did he know about the death of Sir Charles and the phantom hound?

"If it's alright with you, Dr. Watson," said Sir Henry, "I think I'll leave dinner and go straight to bed. I'll have a busy day tomorrow, trying to learn everything about the estate."

We were shown to our rooms and I wished him good night. As I extinguished my candle, I peered out of the window into the surrounding blackness of the moor. The house was bordered by a line of trees, and they were swaying and creaking in the wind. Beyond them, the ground dipped and rolled to the horizon. And above it all, I could see a half-moon breaking through banks of racing clouds. The thought of what might lie in wait for us out there made my nerves tingle. But I knew I must try to rest, so I climbed into bed.

Sleep did not come easily. I tossed around in the sheets, my mind wide-awake even though my body was tired. There was a deathly silence in the house, except for the distant chimes of a clock sounding every quarter-hour.

At last, just as I was about to drift off, I heard a strange noise coming from inside the building. At first I couldn't be sure what it was, but then I recognized it. It was the sobbing of a woman – a loud and desperate sobbing. I listened until it faded away. Then I was left with the clock chimes and the whispering of the wind.

The Grimpen Mire

The fresh beauty of the following morning took away some of the misery from my first impressions of the house. The curtains were pulled back above our breakfast table and the sunlight flooded in. The dark wood panelling of last night was now a golden brown. Even the sinister portraits were brighter and more interesting than I remembered.

"I guess it is ourselves and not the house we have to blame," laughed the baronet, reading my thoughts. "I've got my new country squire clothes on this morning, Watson, and have given my old suit to Barrymore to dispose of. It's time for a fresh start around here. And now we've recovered from the journey, the house looks almost cheerful."

"But it wasn't just our mood that was gloomy last night, Sir Henry," I said. "Did you happen to hear anything unusual during the night?"

His face darkened slightly. "Like what?"

"The sobbing of a woman?"

He stood up from the table and rang the servant's bell. "I did hear something, but I couldn't be sure what it was. It would be best if we settle this straight away," he said, boldly.

When Barrymore entered, he denied any knowledge of the weeping I had heard.

"The house, sir, it makes the strangest noises in the wind. I am sure it was your imagination, Dr. Watson. There is only my wife here, sir, and she didn't make so much as a squeak last night, I can vouch for that."

But he was lying. Walking up to my room after breakfast, I met Mrs. Barrymore by accident on the stairs. Though she tried to cover her face with a hand, I could see that her eyes were red and swollen. Why had her husband deceived us? It was clear she had been weeping. I decided to write a note to Holmes, saying that this Barrymore was a shifty and suspicious character. In fact, both the butler and his shy, sad-eyed wife seemed to be hiding a secret from us. Even within the walls of the house, we might not be safe.

Sir Henry had a pile of paperwork to attend to, so I resolved to go out on the moor and scout around a little. I would walk down to Grimpen village, where Dr. Mortimer had his practice, and try to gather some information concerning our mysterious butler and his unfortunate wife.

It was a beautiful day. The moor, so menacing and fearful a sight to me the night before, was now bathed in sunlight. I walked happily down to the village, which comprised a tavern and three or four little houses. It wasn't hard to find the clinic, where I rang and asked a servant girl if the doctor was in. But he was out on his rounds, so I began the stroll back to the Hall, glad at least that I could work up an appetite for our lunch.

Suddenly, I heard the sound of running feet behind me and I turned to see a small, slim, sharp-eyed man aged between thirty and forty. He wore a light suit and a straw hat and in one hand he carried a large butterfly net.

"Dr. Watson, hold up there!" he shouted. After he had caught up with me, he went on, "Here on the moor we lack the good manners of the city. Forgive me if I appeared rude, hailing you in the open road."

"Think nothing of it."

"You may have heard of me. My name is Stapleton," he said, extending a hand.

"I had guessed who you were from your butterfly net," I said, shaking his hand, which was delicate but surprisingly strong. "Dr. Mortimer had mentioned there was a butterfly enthusiast in the area. But how did you know my name?"

"Oh, I heard that you had called on the doctor and I knew that he had returned with you yesterday. We don't get many strangers around here. How is Sir Henry settling in?"

"Very well, thank you."

"I'm so glad to hear it. There was some worry that he might not want to live out here in the wilds, what with the strange legend connected to the Hall."

I was surprised that he had mentioned the Baskerville family curse, but I did not respond.

"He is not a superstitious man, then?" Stapleton asked.

"I don't think he believes in the story, if that is what you mean."

"But it's amazing," he continued, "just how many of the local peasants believe in these superstitions. Some will even swear they have seen the creature, charging about on the moor."

"People see the strangest things."

"Don't they? Even Sir Charles couldn't dismiss the legend altogether. I think he really believed there was some phantom pursuing him. I have no doubt that is what killed him."

"I don't understand what you mean, sir," I said, slightly annoyed by all this talk of ghosts.

"I imagine he saw some animal loose on the moor, perhaps a sheepdog or fox, and the shock was too much for his poor heart."

"How did you know about his heart problem?"

"My friend, Dr. Mortimer told me."

"You think, then, that some sheepdog chased Sir Charles and he died of fright?"

"Do you have a better explanation?"

"I haven't made my mind up yet."

"Has Mr. Sherlock Holmes?"

This startled me for an instant.

"Oh come, Dr. Watson," he said smoothly, "we have all read those well-known accounts of Mr. Holmes' adventures, published in *The Strand Magazine*. When I came across your name, I guessed that you were the writer. And if you are here, I imagine that Mr. Holmes has been asked to look into the case."

"I am afraid I cannot tell you what progress Mr. Holmes is making."

"Will he be arriving soon, on the moor?"

"No. He is busy with an important investigation in London."

"What a pity," he said softly. But there was something about the man's smile that puzzled me. I couldn't tell if he was sorry to hear the news or not.

"Now," he said, "I would be delighted if you would join me for lunch? I only live a mile or two across the moor and I would like to introduce you to my sister. She has so few visitors these days. Before we came here, I was the headmaster of a little school in the north of England, and she was always surrounded by boys and the other teachers."

"You don't teach anymore?"

"I regret not. There was an outbreak of meningitis

and three of the boys died. After that, we were forced to close. I decided to buy a residence down here, where we could live in peace and I could pursue my hobby of butterfly collecting. We are happy here, but it is a joy for us to have an educated guest for lunch or dinner, now and again. So do please join us."

At first I thought of Holmes' warning that I should never leave Sir Henry alone for too long, but then I remembered the huge pile of paperwork on his desk. He would be busy in his study for most of the day. And while I found Stapleton rather irritating and insincere, Holmes had expressly requested that I investigate all the locals, in case one of them held the key to the puzzle.

"Certainly," I answered, with a smile.

We left the main track and started out along a thin path which seemed to lead to a valley between two hills. At one point I stepped off the track, thinking we could take a shortcut across the moor.

"Watson!" shouted Stapleton, just behind me. "Don't take another step."

"Whatever is the matter?" I asked.

He came over to me and pointed across the open country. "Does it look like solid earth to you?"

"Of course."

"But look," he said, picking up a stone and throwing it a few yards in front of me. As the stone hit the ground, it sank out of sight. "It is a deadly swamp, doctor. It may look like grass, but it will suck you down in seconds."

"How awful."

"We call it the Grimpen Mire. I have seen wild ponies stray into it and slowly sink to their deaths. Once it has you in its grip, there is no escape."

"Is there no safe route across?" I asked.

"Only to a trained eye. In the course of my butterfly collecting, I have mastered the secret paths and walkways that run across it. I did this by memorizing certain landmarks. But anyone unfamiliar with the maze of the Mire would be lost in seconds."

"The moor is indeed a strange and dangerous place, for a visitor. But wait — what's that sound?"

A long, low moan, indescribably sad, swept over the moor. It filled the whole sky and I couldn't tell from which direction it came. It swelled from a dull murmur to a great roar, and then it disappeared.

"The hound," whispered Stapleton.

"But you are an educated man, sir. You don't believe in this superstition, do you?"

"Of course not. I am only telling you what the peasants say it is. I suspect it is a bubbling in the bog, or the rumble of underground waters rising."

"B-but it was a living voice," I stammered.

"Perhaps." he answered. "Oh look!"

No sooner had he cried out than he was running off, into the deadly Grimpen Mire.

"Excuse me, doctor," he shouted over his shoulder, "but it is a *cyclopides*, or I'll eat my hat. Extremely rare. Do not leave the path until I return."

He was bounding along after a small buzzing

insect, hopping from one tuft of grass to the next. I watched him until he had disappeared into the heart of the swamp.

That eerie rumbling in the air had unsettled me. It was unlike any noise I had ever heard, in all my travels. I was sure it was made by a living creature. But then the moor was a strange and unfamiliar landscape to me. I had never seen anything like the Mire. Perhaps the sound was only another odd – but natural – feature of this place.

I turned to retreat along the path, and there before me was a young and attractive woman. She was slim, elegant and tall. I immediately guessed that she was Stapleton's sister, but only because she was out walking in this lonely spot – not because there was any family likeness. She had dark skin while his was light, and her eyes were large and warm, where his were the coldest blue. She stepped close to me.

"Go back," she

ordered, "go back to London immediately!"

"Why should I do that?" I asked in great surprise.

"Can you not tell when a warning is for your own good?" she replied angrily, her eyes blazing. "Get away from here at once. Hush, my brother is coming. Don't say a word to him about this, please."

She began talking of the local wild flowers and the times of year when they should be picked, just as her brother appeared, breathless after his exertions in the chase.

"Hello there, dear Beryl," he cried, although it seemed to me his tone was not altogether friendly. "I almost caught one of the rarest moths in the country." His small, light eyes glanced from his sister's to mine. "And what were you telling Dr. Watson about the local flora?"

"Dr. Watson?" she said in amazement. "But I thought you were Sir Henry."

"No, I am only a common doctor. But I am his friend."

"Then you should ignore what I just said."

"And what was that?" snapped Stapleton.

"Oh, nothing," she said, sounding annoyed, "I was just telling the doctor about the local plants and when to harvest them, but if he is only a visitor the information will not be much use to him."

"No," said Stapleton, "it wouldn't be. Now let's get back to Merripit House for lunch."

"I think," I said, removing my cap for the lady, "that on second thoughts, I should be getting back to Baskerville Hall. But I thank you for the invitation.

Perhaps I can join you later in the week?"

They smiled and said their goodbyes. And, with that, I was picking my way back along the path towards the main road.

Watson Writes Home

Dear reader, over the course of the next two chapters I will present to you exact copies of two messages that I sent back to Sherlock Holmes in Baker Street. These reports, being written at the time of the adventure, are more accurate than my memory can be, all these years later.

> Watson,
> Baskerville Hall,
> November 3rd

My dear Holmes,

I hope that my previous letters and telegrams have kept you up-to-date with all that has occurred so far in this godforsaken place. With each day that I remain here, the moor grows darker and more terrible. But it is fascinating at the same time. When I walk deep into its heart, all traces of modern England are left behind me. Instead, I am surrounded by the stone huts and strange monuments that were constructed by the prehistoric people who once called this wind-blasted place their home. Sometimes, I think that if I were to see a hairy, little man dressed in animal furs darting out from one of these huts, I would feel that he belonged here more than I do. The moor does not seem part of the same world as our comfy rooms at Baker Street.

Anyway, to business...

I am writing today as I have observed something extraordinary, but I shall tell you more of this in a moment. First, I will bring you up to date with the latest developments concerning the local community.

There are now strong reasons to suspect that the vicious killer, Selden, must have left the area. He has not been seen for a fortnight, and the police have announced they are scaling down their search. It's possible he could have taken shelter in one of the stone huts I described above, but with no source of food, and no reported sightings of the man, the police believe it is most likely he has made his way to one of the ports and fled the country.

The moor is so lonely, all the small householders are obviously relieved at the news. Both Sir Henry and I have been very worried about the Stapletons in their isolated house by the Grimpen Mire. Sir Henry even talked about sending the groom over there to guard the house by night, but Stapleton wouldn't hear of it.

I should say, Holmes, that we have been seeing a lot of the Stapletons of late, visiting them for dinner on several occasions. I suspect that the baronet has taken a special interest in Miss Stapleton. I have to admit there is something fascinating and exotic about her, in complete contrast to her cold and methodical brother. He is a hard man to read, Holmes. Despite his apparent self-control, there are times when he gives the impression of hidden fires in his character. For example, one might think he would be pleased at the prospect of a baronet marrying his sister, but more than once I have caught a disapproving, even angry, look on his face when Sir Henry has been talking to her. She is Stapleton's only companion at Merripit House and I guess he would lead a lonely life without her. But it would be terribly selfish if he were to stand in the way of such a fortunate marriage. As to the strange warning she gave me on the moor, she has explained that she was very close to Sir Charles and could not bear to see any harm come to Sir Henry. It was her concern for his general safety, at a time when there are still wild stories told of the killer hound loose on the moor, that made her plead with me (thinking I was Sir Henry) to return to London.

And what of that blood-chilling howl I heard out by the Grimpen Mire? I have decided not to mention it to Sir Henry. There seemed no point in alarming him over something which may turn out to have a simple, natural explanation. I admit that the sound horrified me, but until I have some more facts at my disposal, or a strong reason to suspect that it was made by an animal, I would have nothing to give him but further worries.

Two days ago I was introduced to Mr. Frankland, of Lafter Hall, who made a visit to Baskerville Hall to borrow a book from the library here. Dr. Mortimer, who seems to be the most sociable and well-liked man on the moor, accompanied him. Frankland is an elderly, reclusive man, red-faced and white-haired, who seems unpopular with the locals. He has a habit of taking legal action against his *fellow citizens for the slightest thing. His house is in the very middle of the moor, surrounded by the wildest countryside, and he told me he lives alone and "likes it that way". His only interests seem to be in wine-drinking, literature, court cases and stargazing. He spoke for some time about his interest in astronomy and I understand he has positioned a telescope on the top of his house, to which vantage he clambers at all hours of the day and night. Dr. Mortimer has since informed me that Mr. Frankland takes people to court because he has financial problems of his own. It is possible that these details are of no importance to our investigation, Holmes, but you did ask me to describe all the locals to you, if possible.*

And now I come to my most important discovery.

Last night, around two o'clock in the morning, I was woken by a creak coming from the corridor. I rose from my bed, opened the door and peeped out. A shadow was moving down the hallway and I slipped out of my room in pursuit. I could see the outline of a tall man carrying something, but it was too dark to see who he was. Then, suddenly, he lit a match and held it to the wick of a large candlestick. His face seemed ghoulish and sinister in the light from the flame. It was Barrymore, looking more furtive than I have ever seen him. I swiftly hid behind a large bookcase so he wouldn't spot me.

He followed the corridor into an abandoned wing of the Hall and stopped in one of its bedrooms. Creeping after him, being careful to stay in the shadows, I watched as he walked over to the window and held the candle flame up to the glass. For several minutes he stood there, motionless, peering out into the blackness of the night sky. Then, with

a groan of disappointment, he blew the candle out.

I hurried back to my room and didn't get a wink of sleep all night. This morning, I spoke with Sir Henry and he claims to have heard steps out in the corridor a few times this week, at the same time each night. So, this evening, we are going to stay up and try to catch Barrymore "in the act". Wish me luck, Holmes, for this is a dangerous mission – but a vital one, I believe, for understanding the strange events that have taken place at the Hall.

Your loyal friend,
Watson

The Light on the Moor

Watson,
Baskerville Hall,
November 5th

My dear Holmes,

I have had the most extraordinary adventures since I last wrote to you. In the last 48 hours, things have taken a turn which I could never have anticipated. In some ways they have become much clearer, and in others they have become more complicated. I must put down the facts in the order in which they occurred, so you will be able to sift through them properly.

After breakfast, Sir Henry and I slipped upstairs to examine the bedroom which Barrymore had visited during his night prowlings. The room had no furniture and nothing in it of particular interest. But I noticed that the window looked directly onto the wildest parts of the surrounding countryside. On this side of the house there are no trees to block the view, and I had a perfect vantage point to study the moor and its craggy hills, stretching all the way to the horizon. What had Barrymore been searching for, I wondered, out there on the desolate heath?

"Tonight, by thunder," growled Sir Henry, "we'll discover what's really been happening around my house."

I nodded my agreement. A few minutes later we tiptoed back downstairs, so that Barrymore wouldn't hear us and guess we had been investigating him.

But instead of going through to the library or one of the morning rooms, I was rather surprised to see Sir Henry reaching for his hat and coat in the great entrance hall. So, of course, I donned my own overcoat and cap.

"Not this time, Watson," chuckled the baronet. "Today I am going out on personal business."

"But Sir Henry," I protested, "are you going out on the moor somewhere?"

"I am," he replied, with a cheeky smile.

"You know my instructions. I am not to leave your side. I am sorry to intrude, but I must go with you."

Sir Henry put a hand on my shoulder. "I am sure you are the last man in the world who would wish to interfere with a personal matter, Watson. I must go out alone, and that is final."

And, with that, he picked up his cane and strode out of the door.

For a few minutes I simply didn't know how I should proceed, Holmes, and once more I wished you were by my side to guide me. It was clear that Sir Henry was planning a private rendezvous, and it would have been quite ungentlemanly for me to accompany him. But then I remembered your words. Secret meeting or not, I knew I must protect the baronet. So I raced after him.

After a few minutes quick marching there was still no sign of him. To check I was on the right track, I climbed a low hill and surveyed the countryside. Then I saw him at once. He was down on the moor path that leads to Merripit House, and walking by his side was a woman. I had no doubt as to her identity.

Holmes, I felt terribly guilty standing there, spying on my friend. One moment I thought I should run down there, the next I thought it best to hold back. I could not think of a more testing situation for a gentleman to be in.

I was too far off to hear their conversation, but it was obvious that it was full of passion. She waved her hands and more than once he tried to kiss her. And then, suddenly, I saw something approaching quickly, off to my right. It was the green blur of a butterfly net. And there was Stapleton, charging down on the couple, waving his net and screaming. He had discovered them in the middle of their 'assignation'.

An argument broke out and I could see that both men were bellowing at one another, although the words were too muffled for me to catch them. And then Stapleton took hold of his sister by the arm and dragged her away, leaving Sir Henry standing alone on the edge of the Grimpen Mire. At this point, I was so embarrassed at having witnessed the scene that I ran down the hill and called out to him.

"Watson, have you been spying on me too?" he cried.

His face was still flushed with anger. I at once explained how awkward my situation had been, my duty being to protect him, but my heart not wanting to intrude. Eventually, he smiled and said, "That's alright, old chap."

I asked him what had happened.

"You would have thought the middle of the prairie was a fairly safe place for a man to be private," he said, "but, by thunder, the whole countryside seems to have been here to see me do my courting, and a mighty unsuccessful courting at that."

"You proposed?" I asked, rather shocked.

"I know it's awful quick, but I love her, and I think she might have similar feelings for me. She seems to care about me, Watson. I wanted to ask her today, but she kept changing the subject back to saying I had to leave and I wasn't safe here. I said I couldn't leave the moor without her, and then I asked for her hand. But, before she had a chance to answer, that crazy brother of hers was screaming and abusing me."

"He was annoyed, then?" I said, rather foolishly.

"Like a bear with a broken tooth. I thought he'd be pleased at the match. But he only shouted rude words and then pulled her away – as I suppose you saw. Tell me, why would he act like that? What could it possibly mean?"

But I was unable to offer an explanation.

However, Stapleton did. He came to the Hall a few hours later and was in Sir Henry's study for an hour or more. When he left, they shook hands. He had apologized for his poor conduct and invited us over to dinner at Merripit House the following Friday.

"I still think he's crazy," said Sir Henry afterwards, as we puffed on our cigars in the drawing room. "But I suppose what he said makes sense."

"What was his excuse for his rudeness?"

"He admitted that his sister is everything in his life. She

is his only companion and the thought of her leaving, with any man, was a terrible shock to him. He said he needed some time to get used to the idea. If I don't press her for her hand for the next three months, he will give me his blessing."

"And you agreed?"

"For the hand of Miss Stapleton," said the baronet softly, "I'm prepared to be patient."

So there is one of our small mysteries cleared up, Holmes. We know why Stapleton looked with disapproval upon his sister's admirer. And now I can move on to the next adventure of the day.

That evening, Sir Henry and I waited in his room with a deck of cards and a bottle of good whiskey. We were out to catch the shifty butler, Barrymore. And, sure enough, at two in the morning we heard the creaking boards out in the corridor. We let him pass and then followed after him in silence. He repeated his steps of the previous night and was soon standing in front of the same window, staring out upon the moor. We waited until he had lit his candle and then we seized him.

"The game's up, Barrymore," shouted Sir Henry. "Explain yourself, man."

The poor wretch almost passed out, he was so shocked by our ambush, but he recovered quickly.

"I was checking the latches, sir."

"The latches? This part of the Hall is never used. Is it?"

"No, sir."

"These latches have been locked for years."

"I've still to do my rounds, sir."

"Hogwash!" roared the baronet. "Out with it, man, you heard me."

"So be it," said the butler, with a grim smile. "I knew no good would come of this. It is a secret, but not mine to tell. I can't say anything more."

"Look at this, Sir Henry," I shouted.

While my friend had been questioning the servant, I had been examining the window. Out in the vast blackness of the moor I thought I saw the twinkle of a light. It grew stronger. I held up the discarded candle to the glass and noticed that the light on the moor blinked and then came back, even brighter.

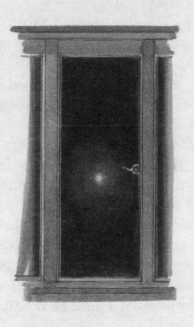

"A signal," I whispered.

"Who is it out there?" barked the baronet at the tight-lipped butler.

"I cannot say," the man repeated defiantly.

"In that case, you will leave my house immediately and in disgrace."

"No sir, don't blame him for all the trouble I've caused," came a new voice at the doorway. It was Mrs. Barrymore, wrapped in a shawl, her eyes streaming with tears.

"It is my brother out there," she whispered.

"Your brother?" I cried.

"My brother, Selden, the escaped convict, freezing and starving on the moor."

We stared at her in amazement. This, then, was the explanation for Barrymore's nocturnal prowlings. This quiet, hard-working woman was the sister of the most notorious killer in the kingdom. She soon told us her story.

"He was a good boy to start with, but we spoiled him and he started thinking he could have anything he wanted in life. Then he fell in with bad friends, thieves and robbers. Each crime led to another, and each was more serious than the last. And at last he lost his mind and started the killing."

"But why is he here?" demanded Sir Henry.

"He was transferred to Princetown, sir, and once there he began making plans to escape. He knew I worked close by and that I wouldn't turn him away if he could break out of the prison. It's the wild country that encourages the convicts not to try to escape, as there's no food or shelter for miles around. When he got out of his cell, he made his way to the Hall and now we look after him. He sleeps on the moor, but he signals to us when he needs food or clothes, and John takes things out to the light and leaves them there. Oh sir, forgive me. I am an honest, Christian woman and I couldn't ignore my own starving brother."

"Is this true, Barrymore?" asked Sir Henry.

"Every word, sir."

"Well, I can't blame you for sticking up for your wife. Forget what I said earlier. We'll talk things over in the

morning."

"Very well, sir." And the two of them left, without another word.

Sir Henry paced over to the window and looked out at the star of light in the distance.

"I wonder," he muttered.

"You're thinking of going out there and catching him?" I whispered.

"Aren't you?"

"It had crossed my mind. He's a dangerous man. The moor won't be safe until he's back in prison. We wouldn't be betraying the Barrymores' trust. After all, we had to force the secret out of them, and we've promised them nothing."

We glanced at each other in the darkness.

"I'm game," we both said, at the same instant.

Minutes later, we were out on the moor. Perhaps it was terribly risky, Holmes, but I have to say, after weeks of feeling powerless, surrounded by the brooding mystery of the moor and the strange legend of the hound, I was hungry for action. I believe Sir Henry felt the same way, watching him charge across the wild heath towards the flickering light.

"Are you armed?" I asked him.

"I have a heavy stick."

"We must attack together and trap him quickly. He will be watching for a trick."

We were a mile out from the house now, crawling over massive boulders and jumping across hissing streams. The moon emerged now and again through thick cloud. But still the light was strong, dead ahead.

And then we heard it...

Out of the vast gloom of the moor came that strange cry which I had already heard out by the Grimpen Mire. It came with the wind through the silence of the night, a long, deep growl, then a rising howl, and then the sad moan as it faded away. Again and again it sounded, the whole sky throbbing with it, wild and menacing. Sir Henry grabbed my hand and turned me to face him.

"My God, Watson, what in this land of horrors, was that sound?"

"I don't know."

"It was the cry of a hound," he whispered. I could feel his hand clasping mine. It was cold as stone.

"It could be anything," I muttered, trying to reassure him.

"What do the locals say it is?"

"They are ignorant people, my friend. Pay no attention to them."

"Tell me," he pleaded.

I hesitated, but could not lie to him. "They say it is the cry of the Hound of the Baskervilles."

Sir Henry groaned and his hand dropped away. "It was a hound," he muttered. "I have good ears from living out on the prairies. It came from over there, from the direction of the Grimpen Mire. Is there some truth to these fantastic stories, Watson?" he asked me. "Is it really possible that I am in danger from a hellhound?"

"Do you want to turn back, Sir Henry?"

I stared around us. We were a good twenty minutes' march from the Hall. All around us was the dark and forbidding moor. Ahead, I saw the convict's light, still gleaming. I confess, Holmes, fear came into me then.

"No, by thunder," roared the baronet. "We'll finish what we came out to do. And if I have to face some hell-dog in the process, then so be it."

I was strengthened by his words. We moved on again, deeper into the night.

There are few things as deceptive as the distance of a far away light on a pitch-dark night. We clambered over the heath towards it, and there were times, Holmes, when I was convinced it was just over the next rock, and other times when it seemed to be miles away, on the line of the horizon. For half an hour we kept pushing closer.

But, suddenly, Sir Henry stopped. Ahead of us there was a little cavern in the rocks, in between two boulders. I could see a candle, jammed into a crack in the stone, protected from the wind. We crept closer.

It took a moment for my eyes to adjust to the light and then I saw him, the strangler, Selden. He was short, but powerfully built. I noticed his upper arms were as thick as a normal man's thigh. He had a thin, sneering face, streaked with the filth of weeks spent living on the moor. He had a thick, black beard, dirty and all stuck together. His eyes were small and cunning, and flicked from side to side, as though peering everywhere for his hunters.

He looked so nervous, I was sure he was watching out for us. Perhaps Barrymore had a special signal to let him know he was coming, and we had failed to give it. I saw him stand to leave and then I yelled, "Charge, Sir Henry." We broke out from our cover and leaped for him. But Selden moved like a cat. In a flash he had hurled a rock in our direction which distracted us for a second. With a terrible curse he slipped out of the cavern, and I saw him dashing onto the heath. We took off after him.

Sir Henry and I were fine sprinters, but Selden was running from the prospect of being returned to prison for the rest of his life. He threw himself across the moor. We kept up the chase for a good ten minutes, but he was gaining on us all the time. At last, Sir Henry stopped and we watched our prey disappear, scampering up the side of a rock-strewn hill. We had lost him.

But it was at this moment that I saw the most amazing thing of that whole, amazing day. I was still panting from the chase when I turned around to glance at the moon. Towering up from the ground was a granite pinnacle (the locals call these strange outcrops "tors"), and standing on top, outlined against the white face of the moon, was the figure of a man. I have never in my life seen anything so clearly. He stood with his legs apart, his arms folded and his head bowed, as if he were watching over the enormous wilderness of the whole moor. It was as though he was the guardian of this place.

It was not the convict. Selden had disappeared on the opposite hill and he was much shorter than this man. I shouted to Sir Henry to turn and look, but when he'd spun around, the figure on the tor was gone.

"Perhaps it was one of the soldiers hunting the strangler?" he suggested, as we trudged back to the Hall.

But I do not think this is likely, Holmes. If it had been a soldier or prison guard, he would surely have come down to speak with us, and not disappeared as soon as he realized he was being observed.

There is a chance that this mysterious stranger may hold the key to the problem of the hound. And if that is too much to hope for, at least he might be able to give us some more information about this whole murky business. If only you could disentangle yourself from your affairs in London and come to my aid, then we might be able to make sense of things. Until you are able, I remain —

Your loyal friend,
Watson

The Man on the Tor

After this strange sighting, events moved rapidly towards their terrifying conclusion. What happened in those last days out on the moor is so firmly stamped in my memory, I can continue from now on without presenting the reports I sent every day to Holmes in Baker Street.

The day after the chase on the moor, a thick fog came down and swirled around the house – and the mood inside was no more cheerful than out. Both Sir Henry and I knew there were dark forces at loose on the moor encircling us. He could not forget the strange howl he had heard, and I was haunted by the puzzle of the mystery man and a feeling of impending danger I was unable to define. What was that animal moan we had both heard? Even if it had a natural explanation, there was the matter of Sir Charles' awful death, the spy in London and the warning note sent to Sir Henry at his hotel. And who was the man on the tor? Was he the same spy we had surprised in the cab in London? Had he followed us here to this grim place, and if so, why? I began to think that the solution to the puzzle must be to catch him. At least he was real and not a ghost. I would be able to grab hold of him, if I could track him down. I decided I would devote all my energy to this purpose. But, for the time being, I kept this ambition a secret known only to Holmes and myself.

I trusted the baronet completely, but I could be sure of no one else in the vicinity. And I didn't want Sir Henry to reveal my plans to anyone in careless conversation. It was possible I was spied upon at every moment in that sinister house, and so it seemed best to keep my intention secret and adopt some of the cunning which I was sure our opponent — or opponents — was using against us.

I began by trying to remember as much as I could about the description of the figure on the tor. Even though I had only had a quick glance at him, I knew he wasn't anyone I had met from the moor's community. He was too tall to be Stapleton and too thin to be Frankland. Barrymore had the right build, but I was certain he could not have followed us and overtaken us in the night.

Indeed, Barrymore came to see Sir Henry in the morning, shocked that we had been chasing after Selden.

"I feel betrayed, Sir Henry," he complained. "I told you about Selden in confidence."

"But, Barrymore," answered the baronet, "you only told us, or should I say your wife told us, when it was forced out of you. And the man is a danger to the public. Look at Merripit House, for example, with no one but Mr. Stapleton to protect his sister from attack. Selden must be put back into his cell."

"Selden is not going to break into anyone's house, sir," protested the butler. "We have made arrangements for him to take a boat bound for South America. He leaves in a few days, and the last thing he wants is to draw attention to himself before she sails. I beg you, gentlemen, to say nothing about him to anyone."

Sir Henry turned to me. "What do you think, Watson?"

I shrugged my shoulders. "If he was out of the country, it would save the taxpayers some money."

"But he might attack someone before he leaves."

Barrymore interrupted, "If he did that, sir, the police would know where he was. He won't bother anyone."

"Well, I suppose, in that case..."

"God bless you," cried the butler.

"And let's hope there's no trouble," said the baronet, glancing over at me.

The butler turned to leave, but hesitated at the doorway. "Sir Henry, I've always believed that one good turn deserves another. You've been kind to me about Selden. There's a piece of information I want to give you. It concerns the death of Sir Charles."

The baronet and I both jumped to our feet.

"Go on, man," shouted Sir Henry. "Do you know how he died?"

"No, sir, but I do know why he was waiting at the

gate. It was to meet a woman."

"Her name?" I asked him.

"I only know the initials, sir. They were L.L."

We took our seats again, and asked the butler to explain how he knew about this extraordinary clue.

"The morning before he died, I noticed that Sir Charles received only one letter. This was unusual, for he was a popular man, and so I paid attention to it. It was from Coombe Tracey, and it had been addressed in a woman's hand. After the death I thought no more of it. But several weeks later, after the inquest, my wife found the ashes of a burned letter in the fireplace of Sir Charles' library. One corner of it had survived. It read: '*Please, please, as you are a gentleman, burn this letter and be at the garden gate at ten o'clock. L.L.*' "

"Where is it now?" demanded the baronet.

"It crumbled to pieces as I read it, sir."

"Why didn't you inform the police?" I asked. "You knew this was important evidence."

The butler shook his head. "I'm sorry, sir, but we had our own trouble then, what with Selden turning up. I didn't want the police around, did I? Anyway, it was after the inquest that we found it. And there's another reason sir."

"Which is?" I demanded.

"It's best to be careful when there's a woman involved."

"You mean you didn't want to damage Sir Charles' reputation?"

"Yes, sir."

"Very good, Barrymore," said Sir Henry. "You may go now."

After the butler had left, Sir Henry could hardly contain his excitement. "We must find her, Watson."

"Do you know a woman with those initials?"

He shook his head. "What should we do?"

"I must let Holmes know at once. It's got to be a vital clue. This will bring him down here immediately, I'm sure of it."

I went up to my room and prepared my report. It had been weeks since I had heard more from my friend than a few words acknowledging that my letters had arrived safely in London. I hoped this new evidence would encourage him to join us without further delay.

The next day there was a storm, and the rain fell down all afternoon, rustling on the ivy and dripping from the eaves of the old house. I thought of Selden, desperate and lonely out on the bleak, shelterless moor, and then I thought of the other man. It must be some strong passion that would drive him to stalk those bare, rocky tors, watching over us.

In the evening, I put on my raincoat and went walking, far out into the sodden moor. I hoped I might find some track or sign of the figure I had seen. The rain was beating on my face and a biting wind whistled around my ears. After an hour of trudging, I found the tor where I had seen the solitary watcher, and I climbed to its top. From here, I could see the twin towers of Baskerville Hall, the

distant lights of Merripit House, and the crude, stone huts of the neolithic people. These were the only signs of life, past and present, in this deserted place. I could find no trace of the solitary man I'd seen two nights before.

As I walked back, I was overtaken by Dr. Mortimer driving his small cart. He insisted I accept a ride with him, as he was coming over to the Hall for dinner. He told me his pet spaniel had gone missing after a walk on the moor, and he had been out looking for him. I thought of the deadly bog at the Grimpen Mire and hoped the doctor's dog was safe.

"By the way, Dr. Mortimer," I said, remembering Barrymore's confession, "you must know all the people around here. Most of them are your patients, after all. Do you happen to know a woman with the initials L.L.?"

"I don't think so. Of course, there are a few families I don't know very well. Oh wait – there is Laura Lyons. But she lives in Coombe Tracey."

"Who is she?" I asked, trying to keep my voice calm.

"Frankland's daughter."

"What? Frankland, the old trouble-maker?"

"Exactly. She fell in love with an artist who was down here doing sketches of the moor. He was called Lyons. He turned out to be a liar and a cheat, and in the end he abandoned her. After that, her father refused to have anything to do with her and stopped her allowance. He had always disapproved of the marriage."

"How does she make a living?" I asked.

"I'm sure Frankland gives her a little. But he's not rich himself, as I've told you. Her story got around and a few of us clubbed together to give her enough money to start a business. Stapleton and Sir Charles helped the most. She runs a typewriting service in the village."

Dr. Mortimer was curious to know why I was asking about Laura Lyons, but I managed to change the subject. I was learning some of the secrecy of my friend Sherlock Holmes, saying no more than I had to, until I was ready to pounce.

After dinner, I retired to the library to drink some coffee while Sir Henry and Dr. Mortimer played cards. But I was soon to have another shocking conversation with the quiet butler. When he came in to refill my coffee cup, I asked if Selden had left on his boat to South America.

"I don't know, sir," said Barrymore sounding slightly desperate. "But I hope he has. I took food out for him two days ago and I've heard nothing since."

"Did you see him then?"

"No, sir," he answered, "but the food was gone."

"So he was definitely out there."

"Unless it was the other man who took it, sir."

I almost spat my coffee out onto the carpet. "You know about the man on the tor?" I managed to say, despite my surprise.

"I haven't seen him, but Selden has. He's hiding too, but he's not a convict. It worries me, sir." His face was almost white with fright. "There's something sinister going on."

"What do you mean?"

"Those noises on the moor, sir, have you heard them?"

"I have."

"They are not natural, sir. There isn't a man I know who would cross the moor at night. There's talk of a dog, a giant dog, with flashing jaws and eyes that spit out flames."

"Don't be silly, man," I said, trying to calm his nerves. But, staring out into the blackness beyond the window, I couldn't help feeling the cold touch of fear in my own heart. Was it true about the hound? I tried to get Barrymore talking about facts again, to bring us both back down to earth. "Tell me about the man, the one that Selden has seen."

"He lives in one of the stone huts, Dr. Watson. Selden describes him as a gentleman, but he can't guess what he's doing out there."

"How does he eat?"

"There's a boy who brings him parcels of food. Selden's seen him walking up from the path that leads to Coombe Tracey. And now I must be going back to the master, sir."

With that, he was gone, and I was left alone to make sense of the mystery. I stared out at the wild night on the moor and promised myself that I would find this stranger by the end of the following day, wherever he was hiding.

At breakfast the next morning, I spoke with the baronet about my Laura Lyons discovery. I felt I had to confide in him as, to interview her, I would have to be away from the hall for most of the day, and I did have a responsibility to protect him. He was very excited and keen to come with me to speak with her, but I thought it might be a more profitable meeting if I went alone. If two men questioned her, she might feel rather intimidated, and I didn't want to risk losing any new information she could give us. Sir Henry agreed a friendlier approach would be better, and I set off for the village without him.

As the Hall fell into the distance behind me, I heard Holmes' voice warning me never to leave Sir Henry's side, and I felt a pang of guilt. I vowed I would do my best to get back to Baskerville Hall before nightfall.

It was easy to find Laura Lyons, as she advertised her typewriter services in the window of the village shop. Her rooms were comfortably furnished, and I was shown in by a maid.

My first impression of her was that she was incredibly beautiful. She had long brown hair and dazzling eyes. But, as I studied her face, I thought I detected a touch of cruelty, and this made me a little suspicious of her. "I have the pleasure," I started, "of knowing your father."

But this introduction was a mistake.

"The pleasure is all yours, sir," she said coldly. "His friends are not mine. If it wasn't for the late Sir Charles and some other kind people, I might have starved for all that my father cares."

"It was about Sir Charles that I have come to see you," I tried again, suddenly realizing that this was a most delicate mission I was on, in this lady's private apartment.

"What about him?" she stammered. I saw her clasping her fingers in her lap as though suddenly nervous.

"You knew him, didn't you?"

"Not really. He was very kind with his donation to me, but we never met."

"What about your letters to him?"

"What are you trying to discover with these questions?" she demanded sharply.

"I do not want a public scandal," I replied. "I thought it was better if I came here to see you, rather than involve the police."

She was silent for a moment.

"Very well. I wrote to him to say thank you."

"And you never met?"

"Perhaps once or twice in Coombe Tracey," she admitted. "But he did not want to be known for his good deeds. He was a modest man."

"How did Sir Charles hear that you needed his help, then?"

"Mr. Stapleton was kind enough to inform him of my situation."

"I see. And did you ever write to Sir Charles asking him to meet you? On the very night when he met his death, for instance?"

"Really, sir, I protest," she said angrily. "Certainly not."

"Then your memory deceives you," I countered. "I could even quote part of your letter back to you." And I did.

She almost fainted as she listened to me recite the end of her letter, but then she recovered herself and sat up straight. "Is there no such thing as a gentleman left in this day and age?" she said, miserably.

"Sir Charles was a gentleman," I told her. "Sometimes paper does not burn as quickly or completely as we would hope. We found part of it in his fireplace. So you did write it?"

"Yes," she sobbed.

"But why did you want to meet him?"

"It was an urgent matter. And I was told he was leaving for London the next day. I had to see him before he departed."

"But I am confused about your request to join him at the gate. Why not go directly to the Hall to meet him?"

She smiled at me. "Do you think a respectable woman could go to a gentleman's house at that hour, sir? The grounds were more... appropriate."

"Well, what happened?" I tried.

"I never went," she spat out. "Someone stopped me from going."

"Who was this?"

But she refused to answer. I questioned her for another twenty minutes, but could not persuade her to confess to me who had intervened in her meeting with Sir Charles.

"But at least tell me why you needed Sir Charles' help so urgently, madam?" I asked eventually.

Again she flushed with anger. "I am married to a hateful man," she snapped. "Every day I face the possibility that he will use the fact that we are married to force me to live with him. But on the day I wrote to Sir Charles, I had discovered that if I could raise enough money to pay certain... expenses, I might be able to get my divorce. I thought that if Sir Charles heard this from my own lips he would help me."

"Tell me, then," I tried a last time, "why you did not keep the appointment?"

"Because," she said icily, "someone else helped me. It was too late to cancel the meeting, so I decided to write with an apology the following morning. When I heard the news, I knew there was no point in any further correspondence. And I will say nothing more about the matter."

She got to her feet and called for her maid. I was shown out of the house, still failing to understand why she would not tell me the other facts I so badly needed. Who had helped her? Who had stopped her from going to the meeting with Sir Charles? She was a beautiful woman, but the slight cruelty I had detected in her expression was enough to convince me she knew more about Sir Charles' death than she was admitting. But for the moment I decided to turn to the other clue I had, and to the moor, where I hoped I would find my answers.

It was my belief that the figure I had seen silhouetted against the moon was the same man Selden had spied on, staying in one of the huts. And I would search each and every one of them until I found him, and then I would force the truth out of him. But, as I drove back towards Baskerville Hall, I realized how difficult my task would be. Out on the moor there were hundreds of these stone huts. I saw a dozen on every hillside, in every valley along the twisting road. To search them all would take me weeks.

I gritted my teeth and promised myself I would begin my search today. I would start in the area around the tor where I had seen the mystery man. Holmes had missed him in London. It would be a triumph for me if I could catch him, when the "Master Detective" had failed.

My first problem was how to send the driver and cart back to the Hall without anyone suspecting my plans. I was determined to keep my actions a secret. Luck had been against us throughout this strange case, but at last it came to my aid. As the cart was trundling past a large house in the middle of the moor, a weak voice called out to me.

"Dr. Watson, is that you? Won't you step down and have a glass of wine with me?"

It was Mr. Frankland, standing at the end of the driveway to his house. Even though my opinion of him was far from friendly after meeting his abandoned daughter, I called to the driver to stop. I explained that I would not be needing him anymore and he should drive straight back to Baskerville Hall. After a quick glass of wine with Mr. Frankland, I could make my way home on foot, visiting some of the stone dwellings on the way.

A few minutes later, I was seated in Frankland's drawing room, sipping from a glass of sherry. Frankland was celebrating. He had just won a court case over a land dispute. I had the impression that he must be a very lonely man, to stop a near-stranger on the highway so he could brag about his victory. He spoke in a high-pitched, nervous voice, and his fingers drummed incessantly on the rim of his sherry glass. I nodded politely as he described how badly he had been treated by the authorities in the court case, intending to say farewell in a few moments and begin my search on the moor. But, suddenly, he said something that made me gasp.

"Yes, the police have been villainous in the whole affair, doctor. If they had treated me better, I would have told them immediately what I had seen through my telescope."

"Oh, and what was that?" I asked, trying not to sound too interested.

"The convict, of course. I have seen his messenger taking food to him."

"Really," I said, my heart sinking for the Barrymores if Mr. Frankland decided to tell the police after all.

"Yes, a young boy who carries a parcel of food each afternoon."

So it was my mystery man who had been discovered, and not the butler. I tried to speak without showing too much excitement. I didn't want Frankland to know that I was depending on him for information. He struck me as the sort of man who would cling greedily to anything once he had decided it might be valuable. "It could have been any boy that you saw," I said casually.

Frankland put his sherry glass down and got out of his chair. His eyes flashed angrily at me, and his white whiskers bristled like those of a snarling cat. "Are you calling me a liar, sir?"

"Why, of course not. I am simply saying that it could be a shepherd boy, for instance, taking food to his father."

"Why would he be taking food to the country around the Black Tor? It is stony and barren, and no good for the grazing of sheep."

My heart jumped. It had to be the mystery man.

"And if you don't believe me," he spat, "perhaps you will believe your own eyes. Follow me to the roof."

We climbed to the top of his house and there, set up so it commanded a sweeping view across a huge swathe of the moor, was a powerful, brass-cased telescope. Frankland hurried over to it. "I am less interested in stargazing these days than I am in the events on the moor," he cried. "You know there is a large reward for this convict. I am tempted to claim it, even though the police are no friends of mine. Now," he glanced at his pocket watch," we might be in luck, doctor. This is the usual time. Ah yes, look quickly before he passes over the hill and out of sight."

I stepped over and stared into the eyepiece of the telescope which he was offering to me. Squinting into the instrument, I could see the shape of a small boy climbing a steep hillside.

"Do you see him?" he cried triumphantly.

I did see him, and I memorized the direction he was heading in. Then I managed to make my excuses, leaving Frankland whining about further court cases and how he would have his revenge on the police. I made my way along the road and, when I was out of sight of the house, doubled back to the moor path, making sure I stayed out of the range of his hungry eye.

The sun was low in the sky when I reached the summit of the hill where we had last seen the boy. Down in the next valley, I saw a few stone huts. One of them still had a roof, and would make a good shelter from the rain and wind. My heart raced when I saw it. The secret of the mystery man was within my grasp.

I crept down to the hut, following a faint path that had been worn in the grass. My nerves were taut with the sense of adventure as I got nearer to the entrance. I threw my cigarette to one side and closed my hand on the butt of my revolver. Then I stepped inside.

It was empty. But there were all the signs I needed to confirm that this was his hiding place. Some blankets were rolled up on one of the stone slabs, where our ancestors once slept. The ashes of a fire were heaped in a corner of the room and beside them I saw some pots, plates and a bucket of water. In the middle of the hut there was a flat stone that served as the table, and on this was the boy's parcel. I unwrapped it. It contained some tins of food and a loaf of bread. At the bottom was a note. I grabbed at it and raised it to the failing, winter light.

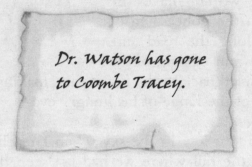

Dr. Watson has gone to Coombe Tracey.

So it was me then, not Sir Henry, who was being watched by this puzzling man. Was it possible that I had been watched since I first arrived on the moor? I remembered the strange sense I had of a sinister presence, spying on the Hall. Had I found its source? Was the man on the tor our deadly enemy, or our guardian angel?

I swore that I would not leave the hut until I had trapped him. I sat in a dark corner, with my revolver ready, and watched the sun go down.

And then I heard his footsteps. It was the sound of a boot clicking on a stone, only a short distance from the hut. I cocked my pistol silently. There was a long pause, which showed that he had stopped, and then a shadow fell across the doorway.

"It is a lovely evening, my dear Watson," said a familiar voice. "I really think that you would be more comfortable out here. Why don't you join me?"

It was Holmes.

Death on the Moor

For a moment or two I couldn't move, hardly able to believe my ears. Was it really him? Then a crushing weight of responsibility seemed to be lifted from my heart. He was here at last.

"Holmes," I cried, moving for the doorway.

"Come out, my friend, and please be careful with your revolver."

He was sitting on a stone, his eyes dancing with amusement as they saw my astonished face. He was thinner than I remembered, his face red and rough from exposure to the harsh weather on the moor. But he was dressed in a suit and his chin was as smooth, and his collar as clean, as they always were in Baker Street.

"I've never been so glad to see anyone in my whole life, Holmes," I cried, shaking his hand.

"Or more amazed," he added. "Well, the surprise is not all one-sided I confess. I had no idea you had found my hideaway until I was twenty feet from the door."

"You saw my footprint?"

"No, Watson," he chuckled. "If you want to outsmart me, you must change your brand of cigarettes. When I see the stub of a cigarette marked 'Bradley of Oxford Street', I know that my friend Watson is in the area. I saw it by the doorway. You threw it down just before you charged into the hut, I suppose."

"I did."

"Knowing you are a determined man, I guessed you would be sitting there in ambush, ready with your revolver."

"I wanted to catch you."

"And so you have. How did you find me? I suppose you saw me on the night of the convict hunt, when I was foolish enough to let the moon rise behind me."

"Yes, Holmes," I said proudly.

"And then you searched all the huts until you found this one?"

"No. Your boy was spotted. I followed his direction."

"Excellent, Watson, well done. You met the old

man with the telescope, I suppose? I saw the lens flashing in the sunlight this afternoon."

He rose from his perch and peered into the hut. "I see Cartwright has brought me a note. Aha... you've been in Coombe Tracey? To see Laura Lyons?"

"Exactly."

"Bravo, Watson. Our work has been running on parallel lines, I see. When we combine forces I expect we shall have a full understanding of the affair."

"But Holmes, what has happened to your blackmail case? The one that held you in London."

"There was no blackmail case, Watson."

"No case? But you said..."

"That was what I wanted you to think."

"Then you have used me, Holmes," I cried, badly hurt that my friend had lied to me. "You do not trust me with your secrets."

"I beg your forgiveness, Watson. I needed to make everyone believe I was in the city, so that I could keep an eye on the case without my quarry knowing that I was hot on his scent. I have been able to work in a way that would have been impossible if I had been staying with you and Sir Henry at the Hall. I needed the cloak of secrecy."

"Even from me, Holmes?" I asked.

"If you had known," he said softly, "that I was out here, suffering in this cold little hut, you would have found it impossible to ignore me. You would have given me away through your kindness. I have been comfortable enough. Cartwright has brought me food and my laundry. I have a loaf of bread and a clean collar. What more could a man ask for?"

"Then my reports to you, they have all been wasted."

Holmes took a bundle of papers from his pocket. "Here are your reports," he laughed, "forwarded from Baker Street, and well-thumbed, I promise you. They have been crucial to my progress in the case."

I was still hurt that he had deceived me, but his praise for my hard work drove the anger from my mind. It was also true that if I had known he was out here, in the wind and wet of the moor, I would have visited him to see how he was. That would surely have led to his discovery by our opponent, whomever he might be.

"That's better," he said, seeing that I wasn't so angry with him, "and now, please tell me what happened when you interviewed Laura Lyons, dear fellow."

The sun had set and the air on the moor had turned chilly. We stepped into the hut to light a fire and get some warmth into our bones. Sitting on hard stone chairs, I told Holmes all the facts about my meeting with the lady who had summoned Sir Charles to his death.

"Hmm," he muttered, "this fills an important gap in my case, Watson. You know, I suppose, that this woman and Mr. Stapleton are on intimate terms?"

"No, Holmes, I didn't," I answered, much surprised.

"There is some kind of secret arrangement

between them, I am sure. It might be a useful weapon when it comes to dealing with Stapleton's wife..."

"His wife?" I gasped.

"Come, Watson. Surely you know by now that the woman who pretends to be his sister is, in fact, his wife?"

"It can't be possible, Holmes."

"Most possible."

"But Sir Henry has fallen in love with her."

"Perhaps he has. But she is still married to Stapleton. If you remember, Watson, Stapleton didn't like Sir Henry getting too close to her, during that private meeting that troubled your sense of good manners so much, did he?"

"But why would she pretend to be his sister, Holmes?"

"Because he forces her to. He knew she would be more useful to him if she were seen as a single woman – and an attractive one. It would help him in his plan."

"What plan, Holmes?"

"Murder, Watson. Refined, cold-blooded, deliberate murder."

Suddenly all my suspicions and ill-feeling about the moor moved onto the cold-eyed Stapleton. It was he, then, who was our enemy in this bewildering case.

"But why, Holmes?"

"My work is not yet complete. I am still unsure of his exact motives, though I have my suspicions. You know that I like to be in possession of all the facts, Watson, before I explain the case."

"So it was she, his wife, who wrote the warning note?"

"I believe so, Watson."

"And that warning to me was a repeat of the note, of course. But how do you know she is his wife?" I asked, still unsure if I could believe this extraordinary news.

"Because, Watson, among all the lies and half-lies he told you, there was a little truth. He was a schoolmaster in the north of England. He has changed his name since then, but by studying the education authority records I managed to find him. It took me a few days, but by using a process of elimination I am now certain of it. Did you know, for instance, that the schoolmaster I finally suspected of being Stapleton happened to be an avid collector of butterflies?"

"So it *is* true," I gasped. "But what does Laura Lyons have to do with it all, Holmes?"

"As a result of your investigation today, I have learned that she seeks a divorce. If that happened, she would be able to remarry. Who do you think she would marry, Watson?"

"Stapleton?"

"Exactly. And when we tell her how she has been cheated, she might be more helpful in revealing the truth to us." He stared out at the moor. "Watson, you have been away from Sir Henry for most of the day. And now it is already dark. Don't you think you should be back at Baskerville Hall?"

I glanced out. All the light was gone from the sky. The hours of darkness had arrived while we had been talking.

"Of course, Holmes. But what does it all mean? What is he after?"

"I've told you, I don't wish to go into the details now, Watson. But, believe me, he is a deadly man and he means to destroy Sir Henry. I am close to trapping him, but he is so clever that he has given me little evidence – and nothing that would stand up in a court of law. There is one, terrible danger that still threatens my plans. If he strikes before I do, all is lost. Your visit to Coombe Tracey today was important, but I almost wish you hadn't left Sir Henry alone. He is in terrible danger, Watson. Wait... what was that noise?"

A scream of horror and pain pierced the silence of the moor. It was so frightening it turned the blood to ice in my veins.

"Oh my God," I gasped. "Who can it be?"

"Be quiet, Watson." Holmes had jumped to his feet and was studying the dark folds of the moor. And then we heard the scream again. It was louder, closer to us, and more desperate than before. I had never heard anything so shocking.

"Where is it? he whispered, and I could tell from a tremor in his voice that even he, the man of iron, was badly shaken. "Where did it come from?"

Once again, that terrible scream came rolling across the moor. This time it sounded closer than ever. And now, there was a new sound mixed in with it. It was a deep rumble, a menacing roar, like a storm-smashed sea. I had heard that sound before.

"*The hound*," breathed Holmes. "Come, Watson!" he shouted. "We must stop it, before it's too late..."

We dashed out onto the moor, our revolvers drawn. But, in the cold gloom, we could see nothing. There was another scream, and then a dull, heavy thud. We stopped and listened, but not a whisper broke the heavy silence of the windless night.

Holmes groaned, "He has beaten us, Watson."

"No, he can't have."

"Didn't I tell you never to leave Sir Henry's side? We must find him."

Holmes ran on into the darkness. At last we heard a desperate whimper and turned in that direction. I could see a cliff, black against the sky, and at the bottom, spread across a rocky slope, was a spread-eagled shape. We dashed towards it.

It was a man, all bent and broken, lying face down on the rocks where he had fallen. He didn't make a sound, and I could tell at once he was gone from this world.

Holmes leaned down and touched him, then pulled his hand back sharply. There was an expression of horror on his moonlit face. He struck a match and I could see his hand was black with blood. The ground was soaked with it, all around the crushed head of the victim. But that was not the worst thing the light from the match showed us. It shone down

on something which made my heart feel faint – the body of Sir Henry Baskerville.

Neither of us could have forgotten that peculiar tweed suit he had worn the first day we met him in Baker Street. The match flickered and died, but there was no need to light another. We knew that our poor friend was gone forever.

"That brute Stapleton!" I roared. "Oh Holmes, I shall never forgive myself for leaving him alone at the Hall."

"I am more to blame than you, Watson," he whispered. "It is the worst disaster of my career. But how could I know he would ignore my warning and come out alone on the moor?"

"Where is the hound?" I cried. "And where is its master, Stapleton? He shall answer for this."

"I will see to that," said Holmes in a firm voice. "Both uncle and nephew have been driven to their deaths by his beast. But now we have to prove the connection between the murderer and the animal. It will not be easy, Watson. Sir Charles was chased, but he died of a heart attack, and Sir Henry has died from his fall, no doubt pursued by the same terrible creature. We have no *proof* of an attacking dog, only what we heard."

"Why shouldn't we go to Merripit House and arrest Stapleton at once, Holmes?"

"Our case is incomplete, my friend. Stapleton is the craftiest and most cunning killer I have ever encountered. Although I have already discovered enough facts to convince myself of his guilt, I cannot yet prove anything about his involvement in the murders."

"So what shall we do, Holmes?"

"We will follow my plan and close the nets on him tomorrow. For now, we must tend to our late friend."

Holmes bent over the body when, suddenly, I feared that he had lost his mind completely. His grief had driven him insane. He started dancing and singing like a lunatic. I rushed over to try to calm him, but he pushed me away.

"A beard!" he shouted. "A beard. The man has a beard."

I turned the body over. The moon was bright enough for me to recognize the face, even though it was screwed up in horror.

"*Selden...*"

And then I remembered that the baronet had

given Barrymore his old clothes when he had first arrived at the Hall. I had thought they were going to be burned or given to a charity, but the butler must have passed them on to Selden. He had taken him clothing as well as food. I quickly explained it all to Holmes.

"Then the gift of clothes was the gift of death," he whispered. "The hound had been given Sir Henry's scent, from the stolen boot I would guess, and so it attacked the man who was wearing the baronet's clothes. That explains it, but there is still a mystery here, Watson."

"What is it, Holmes?"

"How did Selden know the hound was coming for him? We heard three screams. The night is dark and the first scream was several minutes before the last. That would suggest that Selden could see the hound from some distance away. But how could he, on a night as dark as this?"

"Do you remember, Holmes, what the doctor told us in Baker Street? The local people say the hound..." But I was so frightened by the possibility it was true, I could not finish my sentence.

"Go on, my friend," said Holmes, softly.

"They say the hound... it *glows*. They say it shoots out flames from its eyes."

"Do they? I wonder if that is possible, Watson."

"Is the hound always on the moor, Holmes?"

"That I don't know."

"But if Stapleton is behind all this, how did he know Sir Henry would be out tonight? And where could he keep such a beast, where no one could see it in the daytime?"

"There are many questions yet to be answered," said Holmes, mysteriously. "I would say... wait, Watson, what's this? Someone's coming. It's the man himself – he has the daring to come to inspect his work. Not a word, Watson. Don't say a word that betrays your suspicions of him, or my plan for tomorrow will come to nothing."

A man was walking towards us across the moor. I could see the dull, red glow of a cigar between his fingers. It was the butterfly expert, smiling and waving as he came closer.

"Why, Dr. Watson, is that you?" he said softly. "I wasn't expecting to find you out here. But, dear me, who is this? Is someone hurt? Don't tell me... that our dear friend, Sir Henry, has been injured." He rushed past me in his excitement and rolled the body over. I heard a gasp and saw the cigar ember drop to the ground.

"Who is this man?" he mumbled.

"Selden," I said with no emotion in my voice, "the escaped murderer."

For a second Stapleton's face was twisted in surprise, and perhaps disappointment, but then he recovered himself.

"What a shocking sight," he said, coldly. "How did he die?"

"He fell off the cliff and broke his neck," I answered. "My friend and I were walking when we heard a cry."

"As did I," said Stapleton. "It made me worry for Sir Henry."

"Why was that?" I asked, my curiosity getting the better of me.

"I had suggested he come over to our house for a drink or two. When he didn't arrive, I grew worried for him. Did you hear anything else besides the cry?" His eyes were staring into mine.

"No," answered Holmes. "Did you?"

He shook his head.

"What did you mean, then?" asked Holmes. "What else could we have heard?"

"Oh, you know the stories the peasants tell about a phantom hound... I was wondering if there was any evidence for one tonight."

"We heard nothing," I said in a firm voice. "This man has been living on the moor for weeks. He was probably half-mad with exposure and hunger. He was running around in circles, until he tripped over this cliff in the dark."

"I would agree with that explanation," Stapleton muttered, with a sigh which I took to indicate his relief that we were not suspicious of him.

"And what do you think, Mr. Sherlock Holmes?"

"You are quick to recognize me, sir."

"Because we have been expecting you for some time."

"Well, I've no doubt that my friend's idea of what happened fits with all the available facts. I will have to take an unpleasant memory back to London with me tomorrow."

"Oh," he said softly, "you must return tomorrow?"

"I must."

"And has your visit helped you with your inquiry?"

"One cannot always have the success for which one hopes. A detective needs facts. Strange legends and the silly stories of peasants are not of much use to me."

I could see Stapleton staring at my friend, studying him. Then he turned to me. "Perhaps we should cover the poor man's face. The police can come for him tomorrow."

We declined Stapleton's invitation to go back to Merripit House for a glass of brandy, and instead buttoned our coats for the cold walk back to Baskerville Hall. The butterfly collector waved goodbye and then melted back into the darkness.

"The man has nerves of steel," whispered Holmes, as we tramped across the moor. "Did you see how quickly he recovered from the shock of seeing Selden dead before him, instead of Sir Henry, as he expected?"

"It was remarkable."

"He is a remarkable killer, I assure you."

"What will happen, now that he knows you are here?"

"It will make him either more careful or more hasty — we shall see which before too long."

"I would like to arrest him now," I said angrily.

"My dear Watson, you were born to be a man of action. But suppose we did arrest him tonight... I have already told you we can prove nothing. No jury would find him guilty of murder. We can't even prove there is a hound. There wasn't a scratch on Sir Charles. We both know that a dog won't bite a dead man so, when it caught up with him, it didn't leave a mark on his body. By then, his heart had already stopped beating. But what kind of evidence is that? Even if we could find this hellhound, it wouldn't help us to trap its master. Our only chance is to wait for Stapleton to strike, and then be ready to catch him."

"Is there nothing else we can do but wait, Holmes?"

"I look forward to meeting Laura Lyons. She may help us, once we have told her the truth about her fiancé. And I have my own plans, Watson. By the end of tomorrow, Stapleton will be caught in our nets, trust me."

We were at the gates of Baskerville Hall.

"Are you coming in, Holmes?"

"There is no point in hiding anymore, is there. But one last thing before we enter. Please don't say anything to Sir Henry about hearing the hound this evening. Let him believe that Selden fell from the cliff and died. That is not a lie anyway, is it? We must keep his nerves strong for the challenge he will face tomorrow."

"What challenge, Holmes?"

"If I remember correctly, your most recent report stated that the baronet is to join the Stapletons at

Merripit House for dinner."

"What? You would send him into the hands of that man? But at least I am invited to go with him," I whispered, amazed at his suggestion.

"Then you must cancel, Watson, and Sir Henry will go alone. And now, no more on the matter. It is late and I would like to sit down to a good supper. My meals have been... rather crude, lately."

Fixing the Nets

Sir Henry was thrilled to see Sherlock Holmes. Over a light dinner, we explained that he had come down on a late train and had been in such a hurry that he had left his suitcase at Baker Street. The baronet believed our story, and was happy to lend Holmes some items from his own wardrobe.

Before we dined, I had the unpleasant duty of informing Mrs. Barrymore about the death of her brother. She wept into her apron, for she still thought of him as an innocent young boy. Evil, indeed, is the man who has not one woman to mourn his passing.

"You know," said Sir Henry later, over a glass of port in the library, "I've been stuck in the house all day. If it hadn't been for the promise I made to you, Mr. Holmes, I might have had a more lively evening. Mr. Stapleton asked me over to Merripit House, for a glass of champagne."

"I'm sure your evening would have been very lively," said Holmes, with a smile that only I noticed in the flickering candlelight of the room. "But I thank you for not going out on the moor."

"So have you solved the case?" asked the baronet excitedly. "Am I out of danger?"

"It has been an exceedingly difficult and complicated business, Sir Henry, and there is more work to be done. But I will explain everything to you soon, I promise."

"I will help in any way I can," the baronet said firmly.

"Very good. I must ask you to do something that will require great bravery, and I will expect you to do it without question, do you understand?"

"I will trust you, Mr. Holmes."

"Thank you..." Holmes had been about to go on speaking but he paused suddenly, staring off into the distance.

"What is it, Holmes?" I cried.

"Excuse me," he whispered, clearly controlling some excitement. "I was admiring the artists' work displayed on your walls, Sir Henry."

"Oh those?" said the baronet casually. "Barrymore has been teaching me about them. They are the portraits of all the Baskervilles, the whole mob, down through the ages."

"Really?" said Holmes, craftily. "And do you know... who's who?"

"A few of them, though it's pretty complex."

"Who is this sailor then?" asked Holmes, tilting his glass at one of the pictures.

"Oh, that's Rear-Admiral Baskerville," Sir Henry replied confidently.

"And this man?"

"Sir William Baskerville, the politician."

"And this one?" Holmes was pointing at a large portrait of a man dressed in black velvet and lace.

"That man is the cause of all our trouble," laughed Sir Henry. "It's wicked Hugo, who started the legend of the hound."

"Strange," said Holmes. "He is not how I had imagined him. I thought he would be... rougher looking."

"There's no doubt, Mr. Holmes. I have seen the date and his name, written on the back of the portrait."

For the rest of the evening, I noticed Holmes glancing up now and again at this notorious

Baskerville. When Sir Henry had retired to his rooms, Holmes led me closer to the row of portraits and held a candle up to them.

"Do you see anything there, Watson? Describe the portrait of Hugo to me please."

"I see a man in a floppy hat with long curling hair, with a thin-lipped smile and cold eyes."

"Is it like anyone you know?"

"The jaw reminds me a little of Sir Henry."

"Is that all?"

"I think so, Holmes. What are you getting at?"

He brought a chair from the table and stood it next to the portrait. Stepping onto its seat, he lifted the candle in one hand and held his other arm over the top half of the picture. The hat and long hair suddenly disappeared.

"Holmes!" I shouted. "It is Stapleton."

"You see it now, do you?" he chuckled. "I am trained in disguises, Watson. I saw instantly there was a likeness. Stapleton is a Baskerville, without a doubt."

"So he wants the estate?" I whispered.

"Of course."

"But how is this possible, Holmes? Dr. Mortimer said there were no other Baskervilles alive."

"The good doctor was wrong. And soon we will have this new Baskerville in our nets, Watson, trapped like one of his butterflies."

And then he was stepping quietly off to his bedroom. "Now we must rest, Watson," he called behind him. "Tomorrow we will be very busy."

I hurried after him, checking that my revolver was safe and snug in its holster. I had a feeling I would be needing it, before another day had passed.

At breakfast, Holmes explained that he had been up for two hours already, sending some telegrams from the village. The police had been told of the death of Selden, and Holmes had managed to keep the Barrymores' name out of the matter. I was greatly relieved, as I thought they had suffered enough. I thanked him for occasionally being willing to stretch the hard rules of the law. We were soon joined by Sir Henry.

"You look like a general plotting his next battle," joked the baronet, helping himself to some toast.

"I suppose in a way I am," smiled Holmes.

"Then give me my orders."

"Very good. You are invited to dinner tonight, I believe, with the Stapletons?"

"Oh, why don't you come as well," the baronet replied cheerfully. "They're very hospitable people."

"I'm sure they are. But I'm afraid Watson and I are wanted in London, on urgent business."

Sir Henry dropped the slice of toast he had been munching into his cup of tea. "To London?" he whispered.

"Exactly."

"But I thought we were going to solve the case

together," he protested.

"You said you would trust me, Sir Henry. Trust me now. You must tell your friends we are sorry we could not join them, but we will try to be back in Devon as soon as possible. You will give them that message, won't you?"

"I suppose so," said Sir Henry, miserably. "When do you leave?"

"After breakfast," snapped Holmes.

The baronet looked even more disappointed when he heard this last piece of news.

"But perhaps I should join you in London," he cried suddenly. "Wouldn't it be safer?"

"This is your home. You must stay here and do your duty."

Sir Henry nodded his head. "Very well, Mr. Holmes. I am no coward. I will face the danger alone, if you must leave me." He turned to look at me for a moment and I felt a sudden crush of guilt that, this time, not even I would be staying by his side to face the dangers on the moor.

"I have one more request, Sir Henry," said Holmes.

"Name it."

"You will drive to Merripit House, but you must send the cart home. You will walk back after your dinner."

"Walk? Across the moor?" stammered the baronet. "But that is the very thing you've warned me so often not to do."

"Yes I know, but stay on the main path. Don't

leave it under any circumstances. You will be absolutely safe if you do exactly as I say. Do you understand?"

"I do," he answered weakly. "I will do as you say."

"Good," said Holmes, rising from his chair. "Come, Watson, we must get ready to leave." And, with that, he walked briskly off to his room.

I did not speak to Holmes until we reached the station. But once we were standing on the platform, I couldn't contain myself any longer.

"Holmes, this is disgraceful. We are sending that man to his death."

"Calm yourself, Watson," he chuckled. A small boy ran over to us and waited by Holmes' side. "Ah, Cartwright, it's good to see you."

"Any orders, sir?" piped the boy.

"Take the fast train to London," said Holmes, handing the lad a small purse of money. "As soon as you arrive, send a telegram to Sir Henry Baskerville, in my name, to say that if he finds a small notebook I have dropped, could he put it to one side until I return. But first, check if there is a message for me with the station master."

"Yes, sir." The boy darted off along the platform.

"Holmes, I don't understand," I muttered.

"All will soon be revealed to you, Watson," he said with a smile.

"There's a telegram for you here, Mr. Holmes," interrupted Cartwright.

"Excellent," answered Holmes.

MESSAGE RECEIVED. COMING
DOWN WITH WARRANT. ARRIVE
FIVE-FORTY.
LESTRADE

"What does it all mean, Holmes?" I asked again.

"He is the best man at Scotland Yard, Watson. I sent him a telegram this morning. We may need his assistance with the official requirements of the law. And now," he patted me on the shoulder, "I think our visit to Laura Lyons is long overdue, don't you?"

Once in Laura Lyons' rooms, Sherlock Holmes wasted no time in coming to the point. "I am investigating the death of Sir Charles Baskerville," he said coldly. "I want the information which you refused to give to my friend, Dr. Watson."

The young lady stared at him in amazement. "I have nothing to say."

"We already know you had arranged to meet Sir Charles at ten o'clock at the garden gate of his house. We need to know why you didn't keep this engagement."

"And I refuse to say," she answered defiantly.

"I regard this case as one of murder. The evidence

125

may already point not only to your close friend, Mr. Stapleton, but also to his wife."

"His wife!" she screeched, jumping to her feet.

"Indeed. The woman who claims to be his sister is, in fact, his wife."

"You lie," she cried, her wild eyes flashing. "Where is your proof?"

Holmes took some papers from his overcoat pocket. "I have photographs of the couple, taken in New York three years ago. You will see they were using a false name back then, but you will have no problem recognizing them – or the rings on their fingers. These other documents are the statements of witnesses who knew the pair, and a newspaper article concerning the school they ran as man and wife."

After a few moments studying the papers my friend had produced, Mrs. Laura Lyons turned a desperate face towards us. "I have been cheated," she sobbed. "He promised he would marry me once my divorce came through. He has lied to me since the beginning."

"Then do not continue to protect him."

"I will not," she said, angrily.

"Tell me, then," said Holmes softly, "did he ask you to write the letter to Sir Charles?"

"Yes. He even dictated it to me. He said the meeting was the best way to get the financial help I needed to resolve the problems with my divorce. But, as soon as I'd sent the letter, he begged me not to go. He said it would ruin his self-respect if I had to take another man's money. He promised he would find the sum himself. And when I heard of the old man's death, he frightened me into saying nothing about the appointment at the gate. He said the police would suspect me."

"Really? How cunning he is. But you had your suspicions about the truth, didn't you?"

She hesitated, and looked down. "I knew he had a wild temper. But I loved him. If he had been true to me, I would have kept my silence."

Holmes shook his head. "I think you are a lucky woman. For some months now you have been walking on the edge of a precipice, Mrs. Lyons. Stapleton is not the kind of man who would risk leaving any witnesses to his involvement in the affair alive for very long. And now we must bid you good morning, for we have a busy day ahead of us."

And we left her weeping on her sofa.

"At last we have our evidence, Watson," said Holmes excitedly. "We have a motive and a witness. But there is still the hardest task ahead of us, in what could turn out to be the most challenging case of my whole career."

We were walking down to the station and I could see the express train roaring up to the platform. A small, stocky man jumped out from the first class carriage and ran over to us.

"Anything good for me, Mr. 'olmes?" he asked, in a sharp, cockney accent.

"The biggest thing for years. We have two hours, Lestrade. Let's get some dinner into you, and I will give you all the background details. Been to this part of the country before?"

"Never, sir."

"Tonight, you'll get a good sniff of Dartmoor air inside you, inspector — and I doubt if you will forget your visit in a hurry."

The Hound

After several years of accompanying my friend in his unusual occupation, I had grown accustomed to most of his habits. But few of them were as irritating as his refusal to share anything about his thoughts on a case until he had the criminal firmly in his grasp. He once told me that it disturbed his concentration to talk about his methods with "amateurs". He had the whole puzzle set out in his mind, and it only "muddied the waters" to try to explain his thinking. But I also suspect that it thrilled Holmes each time he was able to trap his man, while all others were baffled as to how he had done it. There was a touch of the artist about him. He enjoyed presenting his "work" when it was finished, and not before.

We hired a cart, and sat in silence as it carried us out of the village and climbed towards the moor. Both Lestrade and I had no idea what lay ahead of us, as Holmes had avoided all our questions. Already the night had stolen in on us. My nerves thrilled with excitement and anticipation as the cold wind hit our faces and I saw once more those huge dark spaces of open country. Every stride of the horses and each turn of the wheel was taking us closer to our mission. I felt for my revolver, and snuggled deep into my overcoat. At the entrance to Baskerville Hall, we climbed down from the cart and sent the driver back to Coombe Tracey. Then we set off on the lonely path to Merripit House.

"What's the plan, Mr. 'olmes?" whispered Lestrade. I thought he sounded a little nervous to be so far from the cobbled streets of London.

"A waiting game, inspector," answered Holmes.

"It's not a very cheerful place to wait, is it?"

I could see the policeman shivering, looking around at the gloomy hills and boulders of the moor. Then I noticed there was a huge lake of fog hanging over the Grimpen Mire, making it look even more sinister than I remembered.

"I can see lights," Lestrade muttered.

"Merripit House, the end of our journey. Try to be silent from now on, inspector."

We moved towards the house, but Holmes stopped by some rocks when we were still two hundred yards away from its walls. "This will do," he whispered.

"Here, Holmes?" I asked in surprise.

"Yes, this is perfect for our ambush. Now, Watson, you have visited the house, so please describe the position of the rooms to me. What is that room where the bright light comes from?"

"The dining room."

"Be a good fellow and creep forward to see what they are doing, but do not let yourself be observed, whatever happens."

I did as he commanded. Hunched over, I tiptoed down to the house and peered around the end of the orchard wall, making sure my body was hidden behind it. Through the window I could see two men at a dining table. It was Stapleton and Sir Henry. They were smoking cigars, obviously in the closing stages of their dinner. Stapleton was smiling and chatting, but my friend looked rather nervous. I wondered if he was thinking of the lonely walk across the moor that awaited him, imagining Holmes and I to be safe and comfortable at the fireside in Baker Street.

As I watched, I saw Stapleton get up from the table and leave the room. Sir Henry poured himself another glass of wine. Then I heard the creak of a door and the sound of boots on gravel, moving along the other side of the wall. Once the steps had passed by, I popped my head over the top and saw Stapleton stop at the door of a small hut, in a corner of the orchard. I heard a key turn in its lock, and then a strange scratching noise from inside. After a few minutes had elapsed, Stapleton reappeared and retraced his steps to the dining room. I crept back on tiptoe to join my friends.

"But where is the lady?" asked Holmes, when I'd told him what I had seen. "This is a puzzle."

"Look, 'olmes," whispered Lestrade. He pointed to the dense, white fog, advancing over the Grimpen Mire. In the bright moonlight, it shimmered like an ice field, with the peaks of the far-off tors like distant mountain tops.

"It is moving towards us," whispered Holmes.

"Is that serious?"

"Very serious indeed. It is the one thing on earth that could ruin my plans," he said gravely. "Our success, and even Sir Henry's life, depends on him coming out before the fog traps us."

Above, the sky was clear and I could see thousands of stars scattered like diamonds across black velvet. But just to our left was the wall of thick fog, sweeping towards the house. Every minute it came closer. Soon the far end of the orchard wall was disappearing into the whiteness, and then I saw silver curls lapping at the walls of the house.

"If he's not out in ten minutes," hissed Holmes impatiently, "we won't be able to see our hands in front of our faces."

The fog circled around the house and the lower floor slowly vanished into it. Now all we could see were the upper windows, hanging over the wall of fog like the portholes of a strange ship, floating on a ghostly white sea.

"Should we move to higher ground?" asked Lestrade.

"It will give us more time," answered Holmes. "But we mustn't go too far along the path or something might happen to him before he reaches us."

We dropped back another two hundred yards along the path and took shelter behind a huge rock.

"This is far enough," whispered Holmes. The fog had swallowed the house completely now, and was drifting relentlessly towards us.

Suddenly, Holmes put his ear to the ground. "At last, I think I can hear him coming."

A sound of quick steps broke the silence. We stared at the wall of fog. The steps grew louder and then Sir Henry burst out into open air, like a man jumping from behind a curtain of snow-white cotton. He came towards us, walking quickly, glancing over his shoulder all the time, and then disappeared over the hill.

"Watson," cried Holmes, and I heard him cocking his revolver. "Look out, it's coming."

Something was hitting the ground, quickly, like the roll of a drum. It got louder. The fog had drifted to within fifty yards of us, and we stared into it, waiting for the monster that was about to spring out of it. I glanced over at Holmes' face. His expression was fixed and determined, but suddenly his eyes blinked and his lips parted in amazement. At the same moment, I heard Lestrade scream and saw him throw himself further behind our rock. I jumped to my feet, ready with my revolver, but I was paralyzed by the sight before me.

It was a hound, an enormous, coal-black hound, but not a hound that living eyes have ever seen. Fire shot from its open mouth, its eyes flashed and its muzzle, throat and neck were covered in flames. I could never have imagined anything as savage, as hellish, as the dark shape and snarling face which charged out of that bank of fog.

It was a hound from hell.

Holmes and I fired together. But we had been so shocked when we first saw the beast, it was already bounding past us and closing on Sir Henry. It let out a hideous howl and turned its head to snarl at us. But it did not stop. Up ahead we could see the baronet, his face white in the starlight, his hands raised in horror. The hound was rushing straight at him.

But that howl it let out when we fired proved it was no ghost-dog or legend. One of us must have wounded it, and it had cried in pain. All our fears vanished in a flash. We could hear Sir Henry's screams and the deep roar of the hound and we sprinted towards them. I got there just as the beast had pulled him down and was lunging at his throat, but the next second Holmes discharged five rounds into the animal's side. With a last terrible howl, it snapped its jaws together and rolled to the ground. I held my revolver to its giant head, but there was no need for another shot. The hound of the Baskervilles was dead.

Sir Henry had fainted and it took us a few moments to revive him. Holmes sighed with relief when he saw that the baronet was uninjured. Lestrade pulled a flask of brandy out from his overcoat and held it to Sir Henry's lips.

"My God," said the baronet. "What was it?"

"Don't worry, it's dead. We have laid the family ghost in its grave, once and for ever."

I examined the hound. It was a huge creature, perhaps an English mastiff crossed with a bloodhound. Its huge jaws seemed to be dripping with flame and its small, burning eyes were ringed with fire. I placed my hand on its coat. As I lifted my fingers, I noticed how they gleamed and sparkled in the darkness.

"Phosphorus," I whispered. "The dog has been smeared with the chemical to make it glow."

"Yes," said Holmes next to me. "In fact, it must be a very cunning mixture of chemicals. Phosphorus is very pungent. But this paint has no smell to put the dog off his scent. I was ready for a hound, but I didn't expect it to look so terrifying. Forgive me, Sir Henry, for exposing you to this horror."

"I can only thank you, Mr. Holmes, for saving me."

"Are you strong enough to stand?"

"Give me another sip of brandy and I'll be ready for anything," answered Sir Henry. "What do you want me to do?"

"You've had a bad fright, dear fellow, and I want you to rest. Stay here for the moment, until you feel stronger. I will leave you my revolver, freshly loaded, in case of any new danger. We will return soon and escort you back to Baskerville Hall. Our job isn't quite finished yet."

We started back into the fog towards Merripit House.

"Stapleton will have fled," whispered Holmes. "Our shots will have warned him that the game's up."

"The fog might have muffled the blasts," I suggested.

"Perhaps, Watson. But he would have followed the hound to make sure it finished off its victim, so I think he would have been too close not to have heard the revolvers. But we must search the house to make sure."

The front door was open and we dashed inside. Holmes grabbed a candle and began scouring the house. There was no sign of the man we were chasing. But there was a sudden clunk from one of the upstairs rooms.

"Come on," shouted Holmes. We tore up the stairs. One of the bedrooms was locked, but we broke down the door and charged in.

The room was like a small museum, the walls lined with glass cases, housing Stapleton's butterfly collection. There were hundreds of insects, neatly pinned to cards in careful rows. But this was not the most startling sight in the room. Directly before us, tied to one of the heavy, upright beams, was a figure in ragged, torn clothes. It was Mrs. Stapleton. As we untied her, I saw a web of red marks across her neck, the lashings of a whip. She fell into my arms.

"The brute, Holmes, he's tortured her. Lestrade, give me your brandy."

When she had regained enough strength she asked, "Is he safe? Has he escaped?"

"We will catch him," promised Holmes.

"No, no," she cried. "I don't mean my husband. Is Sir Henry safe?"

"Yes."

"And the beast?"

"Dead."

She gave a long sigh of satisfaction. "He deserves

my hate," she said angrily. "See how he has treated me." She showed us her arms, which were covered in terrible bruises. "But the real torture has been in my mind. I could put up with everything, the lies, the solitude and deception, as long as I thought he loved me. But tonight I saw that he cared nothing for me." She sobbed passionately as she spoke.

"Tell us where he is. Help us now and you will make it up to Sir Henry."

"He must be on the Mire," she laughed. I was shocked to see the change in her expression. It was as though she was thrilled to realize that her husband might be out in that deadly bog. "There is an old tin mine on an island in the middle of the swamp. He has a secret base there. That's where he'll be."

Holmes stared out at the white fog licking at the window pane. Mrs. Stapleton laughed again and clapped her hands together. "Yes," she screamed, "he will lose his way in this mist. How could he see the guide posts we planted on a night like this? We used them as landmarks to show us the way across the Mire, but it will be impossible to see them in all this fog."

We decided it was useless to chase after the murderer until the weather had cleared. Leaving Lestrade to guard the house and its mistress, Holmes and I set off to walk the baronet back to Baskerville Hall. He responded bravely to the news that the woman he loved was Stapleton's wife. But as I explained how Stapleton had been our deadly enemy, I could tell from Sir Henry's glazed expression that he was already in the first stages of shock. His nerves had been badly damaged by the attack on the moor. Within hours, he was in the grip of a terrible fever and I had to summon Dr. Mortimer to care for him. It would be a long time before Sir Henry would be the same, happy-go-lucky adventurer we had met only a few weeks earlier in Baker Street.

The next morning, the fog had lifted and Mrs. Stapleton guided us to the edge of the Mire. She pointed out the first of the guide poles they had planted in firm ground, to show a route across the bog. We zigzagged our way across the swamp, following the poles. The bog stank of rotting plants and worse, and each wrong step plunged us up to our thighs in thick, sucking mud. The Mire seemed to tug at our feet as we stepped over it. At last we saw a sign of life, a dark object stuck in some reeds a few yards off the path. Holmes sank to his waist in the slime when he tried to grab it, and if Lestrade and I had not been there to pull him out, he would never have survived. He held an old leather boot in the air.

"It was worth the mud bath," he announced proudly. "It is Sir Henry's missing boot, thrown away by Stapleton as he was running to escape us. He did use it to give the hound the scent, as I suspected."

"So we know he got this far safely," I muttered.

But we were never to know the truth of what happened to that desperate man. When we reached the island at the heart of the Mire, we searched everywhere for clues, but there was no trace of Stapleton. I stared out at the miles of bog surrounding us.

"He is in there somewhere," whispered Holmes at my side. "I know it, Watson. He is buried in that foul, stinking, bottomless pit, buried forever."

We searched the tin mine for further evidence of the hound and its master. In one of the crumbling buildings, we found a heavy chain and a pile of gnawed bones. A small skeleton with brown fur lay among them.

"Mortimer's spaniel," I whispered, remembering how I had met him looking for the unlucky creature on the day of the storm.

"Look, Watson," cried Holmes. He was holding an old paint can, its sides splashed with the strange mixture that Stapleton had rubbed into the dog's coat.

"The mystery clears a little," he explained. "He could hide his hound here, but he couldn't keep it quiet. That explains the howls you heard, even in the hours of daylight. This luminous paste shows a touch of genius. It made the dog look like the hellhound described in the legend, and it also made certain that no curious peasants would dare to come too close if they saw the dog, away in the distance. No wonder the convict ran over that cliff, Watson. He must have seen the hound coming for him from a long way off and had time to work himself up into a mad fear. The same was true for poor Sir Charles, of course."

"How awful, Holmes," I muttered.

"And now the murderer lies out there," said my friend, pointing to the Mire. "Come, Watson, it is time we were going home."

The Case Concluded

A month passed before I was able to question Sherlock Holmes about the strange case of the Baskerville hound. As soon as we returned to London from Devon, we were involved in a dangerous and exhausting puzzle to find a missing treasure, and knowing that Holmes would never allow his mind to wander from whichever case he was presently involved in, I decided to be patient.

One cold and stormy night, we were sitting either side of a blazing fire in our rooms at Baker Street, and I asked my friend if he would go over the details of the case for me. That same afternoon Sir Henry and Dr. Mortimer had called on us. The doctor had decided that the best cure for the baronet's shattered nerves would be a round-the-world voyage, and they were leaving for Naples the next morning, as their first port of call. Seeing our old friends had reminded Holmes of our adventure on the moor, and he seemed happy to talk it over with me.

"Well," he drawled, "I have been fortunate enough to have had two conversations with Mrs. Stapleton since the night we shot the hound, and I now believe I have a full understanding of the matter."

"Could you outline it for me, Holmes?" I asked. "For my records?"

"Oh yes," he replied, "you have your readers to think of. Well, the case begins with examining the motive. My inquiries have shown that the portrait did not lie and that Stapleton was indeed a Baskerville. He was the son of the scoundrel Rodger Baskerville, who had fled years before to South America. Dr. Mortimer was told that Rodger died unmarried and childless, but both of these statements were untrue. He did marry and he did have a son, who shared his name.

"The son married Beryl Garcia, said to be the most beautiful woman in Costa Rica. It seems he then stole a considerable sum of money from the government bank, changed his name to Vandeleur, and slipped back to England with his wife. He set up a school in the north of the country, but it soon fell into disrepute and went bankrupt. He then changed his name again – to Stapleton – and arrived in Devon with the remains of his stolen money and a taste for butterfly collecting. I have been to the British Museum, Watson, and they tell me 'Vandeleur' is famous in the butterfly world and is credited with discovering several new species."

"As soon as Stapleton arrived in Devon, he began making plans to seize the Baskerville estate from Sir Charles. I do not know when he learned that there were only two men between himself and fantastic wealth, but the fact that he encouraged his wife to pretend to be his sister indicates that the plot was in his mind from an early stage.

"He took a house close to the hall and he made friends with Sir Charles. It was the baronet himself who told Stapleton the legend of the hound. From his conversations with Dr. Mortimer, Stapleton learned Sir Charles' heart was weak, and so, with a criminal ingenuity approaching genius, he made up his mind to scare the baronet to death. All he needed was a dog that looked as though it had jumped straight from the depths of hell.

"He bought the largest hound he could find, from Ross and Mangles' pet shop in the drab suburb of Fulham, London. I have been there and spoken with the manager, and he tells me the dog was the strongest and most savage he had ever seen. Stapleton brought it back on a train, but he got off at a station on the other side of the moor and walked the last fifteen miles across country, to make sure he wasn't spotted. On his butterfly hunts he had already discovered the paths that lead to the heart of the Grimpen Mire and found the old tin mine there. He decided this would be the safest place to hide the hound until his chance came to terrify Sir Charles.

"But it was some time coming. The baronet was so nervous he would not leave the Hall at night. Stapleton lurked around the grounds with his hound, waiting for his prey to come out for a walk. This is when the dog was sighted by a few peasants. Even Dr. Mortimer might have seen it. Do you remember the 'black bull' he described glimpsing at the end of the drive, Watson? The stories of a demon dog on the moor began to spread. But, of course, this only made Sir Charles even more frightened of leaving his house.

"Stapleton hoped to use the charms of his 'sister', to tempt Sir Charles to come out to Merripit House at night, but she wanted nothing to do with the plot. Even with violence — the bruises we saw — she refused to help. And this is where we come to Laura Lyons.

"Claiming he was a single man, Stapleton seduced her and promised he would marry her as soon as she divorced. When he heard that Sir Charles was leaving for London, he realized he needed to act urgently. So he encouraged her to send her letter, asking the baronet to wait at the gate. Stapleton then persuaded her not to keep the appointment. And then he struck.

"He rushed back to the Grimpen Mire for his hound, smeared it with the special paint and then brought it over to the side gate at Baskerville Hall. Ready with some piece of Sir Charles' clothing, no doubt, Stapleton gave the hound the scent and let it loose. The dog raced across the moor and sprang over the gate towards the horrified Sir Charles. Then it chased him down the yew-tree avenue. Imagine the scene, Watson. In that gloomy tunnel of trees, a huge, black hound with flashing jaws is snarling at your heels. Sir Charles' heart could not bear it. The dog caught up with him, but by then he was already dead, and so it only sniffed at the body before running back to its master."

Holmes nodded his head, deep in thought. "It was a cunning and incredible plan, Watson. The real killer was fear. Or was it the hound? Stapleton hadn't lifted a finger against Sir Charles and, once he got rid of his dog, there was no way of linking him to the murder. His only weakness was Laura Lyons, who must have been suspicious, and his wife. But both she and Laura Lyons loved him. Stapleton used this power over them to keep them silent, so for the moment, he was safe. And then came the problem of Sir Henry."

Holmes lit his pipe and puffed at it thoughtfully. "As I have said before, I am not sure how or when Stapleton learned of the existence of Sir Henry. It's possible he thought Baskerville Hall would be his as soon as he had murdered Sir Charles. But we know Dr. Mortimer told him there was an heir a few days after the murder, and so he had to make new plans. By this stage he had already killed, and he was ready to go on killing to make sure he got his inheritance.

"Stapleton came to London thinking there might be a way to get rid of Sir Henry even before he journeyed to Devon. But he had to bring his wife. By now he couldn't trust her completely, as she had resisted him over the tempting of Sir Charles. He dared not leave her too long out of his sight. So he locked her into their hotel room while he followed us in the cab, waiting for a chance to strike, but she was able to make the warning note.

"I now suspect," Holmes added, waving the stem of his pipe at me, "that she made the note out of newspaper cuttings, in case Stapleton discovered it – or in case Dr. Mortimer ever showed it to him. She was disguising her handwriting from her husband, not from us."

I shook my head in sympathy for the poor woman who had risked her life sending Sir Henry her warning.

"In London, he made his first mistake," continued Holmes with a smile.

"What was it?"

"The boot, Watson, the boot. As soon as I heard that Sir Henry had lost a boot, I was suspicious. But when I heard that a second boot had been taken, one that would bear the scent of its owner when a new boot would not, my suspicions were confirmed. I knew we were dealing with a real dog. Devil dogs don't need the scent of a man. I believe it is often the strangest or smallest detail, Watson, as I remarked to you some time ago, that is the most important in understanding a case."

Holmes refilled his pipe and lit it slowly. "Then we come to my mistake with the cab. He recognized me Watson, as I crossed the street towards him. The fact that he knew me, combined with the criminal expertise he displayed throughout this case, makes me suspect that Stapleton had been involved in crime for some years before we had the pleasure of meeting. There have been four daring robberies in Devon in the last two years. I now wonder if Stapleton was behind them?"

"And what happened to the hound when its master was in London?"

"You cannot catch me out so easily, Watson. There was an old servant at Merripit House whose name, I was told, was 'Anthony'. I have tracked him back to the school that Stapleton ran, and so he must have known the couple were man and wife. This man has vanished, Watson. I believe he may have left the country. Mrs. Stapleton did not want to discuss him in my conversations with her. She said he was a loyal servant, and I think she was trying to protect him. But she did make the mistake of calling him 'Antonio' once, while we were talking. That is a common name in Central America."

"You think he's another Costa Rican?" I blurted.

"Exactly, Watson. I believe this man would have cared for the hound when Stapleton was absent. It is possible, of course, that he knew nothing of his master's deadly intentions."

Holmes knocked out the ashes from his pipe and

settled back into his leather armchair. "And then the chase moved back to Devon. But before I go on, Watson, I would like to add a word or two about my methods of investigation – only to make things clear for your readers, of course."

"Of course, Holmes," I replied, jokingly.

"Do you remember when I examined the warning note?"

"I think so."

"Do you remember anything peculiar about my examination?"

"I don't think so," I said, casting my mind back. "I remember you holding it very close to your face."

"To my nose, in fact, Watson. The lady may have disguised her writing, but she forgot to disguise her perfume. I know of seventy-five perfumes which a good detective should be able to recognize. Her choice was a rare one, known as 'White Jasmine'."

"But how could that help the case, Holmes?"

"Because, my friend," he explained, "before I had even left my armchair I suspected we were dealing with a woman. How many women did we know of, living close to Baskerville Hall?"

"Only Mrs. Barrymore and Mrs. Stapleton."

"Precisely, Watson. And a servant woman would never be able to afford 'White Jasmine'. So I suspected Mrs. Stapleton and her brother, and I suspected that they – or, I should say, one of them – was using a real dog. How far from the truth was I?"

"I am amazed, Holmes. You were already so close to solving the puzzle."

"It is quite elementary, my dear Watson. Facts and deduction. Now back to our case."

"I wanted to watch Stapleton without showing myself," Holmes continued, "and that is why I had to tell you I was too busy in London to join you. Again, I apologize for the deception."

"Apologies accepted," I said with a bow of my head.

"My hardships were not too severe and a true detective should be prepared to put up with much worse. Most of the time, I stayed at the Coombe Tracey tavern. I only used the hut on the nights when there was the promise of action. I had all your reports forwarded to me from Baker Street, so none of them went to waste. And they were crucial to my investigation, Watson.

"From your letter, I learned about the Stapletons' school, and this was how I went on to discover they were man and wife. By the time you surprised me at my hut, I already knew most of the facts, but I was not in a position to arrest the man. We had to risk the life of our client in order to kill the hound and catch Stapleton red-handed. I confess I was surprised by the fog and the way the hound burst out of it, its jaws flashing flames in the darkness. I wasn't expecting that, and my lack of forethought almost cost us Sir Henry's life. But I have been told by Dr. Mortimer that he expects the baronet to make a full recovery. It will take time for his nerves to heal..."

"And his broken heart," I added.

"Indeed, Watson. But Mrs. Stapleton has suffered terribly as well. She tried to warn Sir Henry away twice, and she refused to have anything to do with the hound. For these reasons I am convinced she is a good woman. She went along with most of Stapleton's wishes because she loved him. I also suspect she feared him – and wisely, as he was a dangerous man. But when he used the baronet's love for her to lure him out onto the moor, she protested so much that Stapleton had to tie her up and gag her. Perhaps Stapleton was hoping he could win her back, once the estate was his. Perhaps she could have had... a much darker future."

"But Holmes," I asked, "how could Stapleton claim to be a Baskerville and inherit the estate, if he'd been living under another name all this time, only a few miles distant?"

"Another good question, Watson. Mrs. Stapleton has told me that her husband had come up with three possible schemes to claim the money. He could have approached a lawyer back in Central America, and produced documents proving who he was. The lawyer could then have transferred the money from the estate without Stapleton ever having to show himself in England. Once he had the money he could have returned to Devon if he wanted, perhaps even posing as the new buyer of Baskerville Hall."

"The cunning devil," I whispered.

"And you should remember, Watson, he was an expert at disguise. He could have visited London in disguise and claimed the estate that way. His third choice would be to hire an accomplice to claim the money. Stapleton would give him all the proper documents and enough money to buy his silence. He was a desperate man, Watson. He would have found a way in the end."

"Yes, Holmes. But now he lies at the bottom of the Grimpen Mire. There is no way he could have escaped it."

"I think we've said enough about this terrible business," Holmes said, getting up from his chair. "It is time to think of something more cheerful. I have reserved a box at the opera, Watson. If I can trouble you to be ready in a dinner suit, in thirty minutes or so, I think we'll have time to stop for a little dinner on the way."

And, with that, Mr. Sherlock Holmes picked up his violin, closed his eyes in concentration, and began to play.

About Conan Doyle

Arthur Ignatius Conan Doyle was as complex and intriguing as his famous literary creation, Sherlock Holmes.

He was born in Edinburgh on May 22nd, 1859 and trained there as a doctor. His fellow students included the budding writers, J. M. Barrie and Robert Louis Stephenson, but it was a medical professor who was to make the greatest impression on the young Conan Doyle.

Dr. Joseph Bell studied the physical character of his patients and made deductions about their trade, lifestyle and habits. He taught his students the importance of observation, to help the doctor discover the patient's background. Little did he know that a few years later Conan Doyle would take this observational skill and adapt it to solving crime, in the form of Sherlock Holmes.

At twenty, Conan Doyle received his medical degree and had his first taste of adventure, when he took a job as ship's surgeon on the whaling boat *Hope*. He was always to retain his love of travel and sporting activity, being a keen skier, cricketer and golfer. After establishing himself as a doctor in the south of England, he began submitting short stories to magazines. The first Holmes adventure, *A Study In Scarlet*, was published in 1887, but it wasn't until the *Strand* stories started to appear in 1891 that the character became a sensation.

There were 60 adventures in total. Among the most popular were *The Sign of Four*, *The Five Orange Pips*, *The Speckled Band*, *The Engineer's Thumb*, and *The Naval Treaty*, all published between 1890 and 1893.

Conan Doyle was a prolific writer. Aside from Sherlock Holmes, he created two other famous characters: the eccentric explorer, Professor Challenger, in *The Lost World* (1912), and a dashing officer in the Napoleonic wars, Brigadier Gerard, in *The Exploits of Brigadier Gerard* (1896). They were well-received by the public, but could never eclipse the popularity of the Baker Street detective.

The author was interested in politics, standing twice for a government position, and was also a gifted historian. He received a knighthood in part for a book he wrote covering the events of the Boer War. But his greatest interest lay in matters quite opposed to the scientific precision of Holmes. Conan Doyle was fascinated by the world of the paranormal, the "unexplained".

Throughout his life, he enjoyed friendships with some of the leading investigators into this topic, including Harry Houdini, the renowned escapologist and paranormal disbeliever. But, as he grew older, Conan Doyle's growing passion for the subject alienated many of his supporters, who had loved the hard, scientific judgement of Holmes. He toured the world giving lectures about contacting the spirit world, and he was involved in a number of scandals. A famous case was that of the "Cottingley Fairies", when two young girls claimed to have taken pictures of tiny fairies at the end of their garden, in Cottingley, in the north of England. Conan Doyle examined the pictures and declared the fairies were real. He even wrote an article called *The Coming of the Fairies*, published in a national magazine in 1928. But many people remained sceptical and the pictures were eventually shown to be fakes, the result of tricks with cut-out figures and double exposure on the camera film.

The incident irreparably damaged the reputation of the author, and he was to die only a few years later, on July 7th, 1930. But, by then, Sherlock Holmes was more famous than the man who had created him. Conan Doyle will be remembered for many achievements, but none so great as his violin-playing detective.

Films

There have been over twenty film adaptations of *The Hound of the Baskervilles*. Listed below are some of the more interesting versions.

The Hound of the Baskervilles (1932) — the first "talkie". Made by Gainsborough Pictures.

The Hound of the Baskervilles (1939) — perhaps the most famous production, featuring Basil Rathbone, considered by many Sherlockians to be the finest portrayal of Holmes.

The Hound of the Baskervilles (1959) — made by Hammer Studios, best-known for making horror films, and starring two actors who would later become renowned for their horror-film performances, Peter Cushing and Christopher Lee.

The Hound of the Baskervilles (1978) — a comedy Holmes, with Peter Cook and Dudley Moore. Some critics have claimed, "It's so bad it's funny."

The Hound of the Baskervilles (2002) — a BBC film that uses impressive "animatronic" special effects for the hound.

Dr Jekyll & Mr Hyde

From the story by
Robert Louis Stevenson

*Behind the locked door of Dr. Jekyll's laboratory lies
a mystery his lawyer is determined to solve. Why
does the doctor spend so much time there? What is
the connection between the respectable Dr. Jekyll
and his visitor, the loathsome Mr. Hyde? Why has
Jekyll changed his will to Hyde's advantage? And
who murdered Sir Danvers Carew?*

This spine-chilling retelling brings Robert
Louis Stevenson's classic horror story to life,
and is guaranteed to thrill and terrify modern
readers as much as when *The Strange Case of
Dr. Jekyll and Mr. Hyde* was first published over
a century ago.